Enchanted Entrapments

EDITED BY JADE CINDERS

Enchanted Entrapments

EDITED BY JADE CINDERS

Enchanted Entrapments

Paperback edition ISBN: **979-8-9851865-0-5**
Electronic edition ISBN: **979-8-9851865-1-2**

Published by Madhouse Books
Spring Valley, California
http://www.MadhouseBooks.com

First Edition: November 2021

TABLE OF CONTENTS

Preserve By Aric Sundquist   1

The Fairie Ring By Lilla Glass   11

The Drive By Victor Nandi   27

The Watcher on the Mountain By Cory Mason   39

She Who Binds the Bones By M.S. Swift   50

Victim By Naomi Brett Rourke   69

Mountain Song By Mark Towse   77

The Carriage By N.E. Salmon   91

Ata Nor By Michael A. Wexler   106

Her Muse By Kay Hanifen   116

Seasons End By C. Marry Hultman   130

The Shard By William Tudor   152

Lost Sleep By Bernardo Villela   167

The Untamed By Toshiya Kamei   189

Stone and Wood By Sergio Palumbo   203

PRESERVE

BY ARIC SUNDQUIST

Charles Neese listened to the tree-speak early each morning. It usually happened when the sun crested the horizon and splashed warmth across the woods, causing the trees to communicate in secret whispers, or "sermons," as he liked to call it. The language itself sounded quite odd— mostly a series of clicks and pops that reminded him of a dog lapping up water from a mud puddle. Although he couldn't understand the words, he loved listening to the sounds.

With his electric drill, he bored a hole deep into the nearest tree, then hammered the metal tap inside, ensuring the angle allowed the sap to flow freely. He attached a plastic collection bag underneath and propped a cover over the top, preventing rainwater and snow from polluting the contents. Sometimes, he collected so much sap the bags resembled bloated wood ticks siphoning blood from their deciduous hosts.

He tapped a dozen more trees, then checked all of them one final time to make sure they were set up properly. By this time, the sun was getting high in the sky, and hunger was gnawing at his insides. He gathered up his tools, started his four-wheeler, and headed back home to his cabin.

In forty-five years of living in Michigan's Upper Peninsula, he had never seen such a strange winter. The snow had begun in the middle of December and stopped in mid-February. Usually, the region was hit with snow from November until April and measured, on average, two hundred inches annually. Strangely, this year barely hit thirty inches. It was now mid-March and felt like the beginning of summer.

Back home at his cabin, he threw a couple of logs into the fireplace and stirred the cooling embers back to life, then busied himself making lunch using a portable electric skillet powered by a car battery. He cooked scrambled eggs and French toast and five strips of bacon and poured maple syrup over everything. He wanted more bacon, but his doctor had warned him against eating so much red meat. He was already fifty pounds overweight.

Charles ate slowly, contemplating a plan of action for the rest of the day. If he couldn't get his usual five-hundred gallons by the end of the week, he'd be in serious trouble. He had a dozen orders to fill at local restaurants. His other business was a snow removal service, but since the snowfall was cut so short this year, his job had proven meaningless, the money negligible. He was counting on a good syrup harvest to make ends meet.

He finished his meal and decided to go for one last drive around his property. He threw on his gear and hopped back on his four-wheeler, then cruised through the backwoods, stopping to check on his collection bags scattered throughout the trees.

Unfortunately, they were all empty.

He needed to figure something out, and fast.

Charles arrived at the fence later that day. He had discovered it three years ago, shortly after acquiring the land at auction. To this day, he didn't know who owned the property on the other side. The fence was ten feet high, and it stretched on and on for miles.

Charles crept up closer to the fence posts. He slipped to his knees and peeked through a gap between the support boards. In the past, every time he did this, an involuntary sigh escaped his lips. This time was no exception.

A lush forest untouched by civilization stood on the other side of the fence. The trees loomed like giants stretching leafy arms toward the heavens. Spring grass bloomed from the dark soil, reminding him of a picturesque scene from Ireland or Scotland. He even imagined a decrepit castle hidden deep within the forest canopy. It was beautiful, pristine country, unlike anything he had ever seen.

He knew he had to return home and rest up for the long day tomorrow, but he didn't want to leave yet. He wanted to stare at the beautiful landscape. It felt like looking through a doorway to another world.

Finally, regretfully, he tore himself away and walked back to his four-wheeler. He clicked on the ignition and revved the motor a few times to prevent the engine from flooding, and then he drove away. As he rode home, he decided on a new course of action.

The following day, Charles put in a call to the Green Haven County Clerk's office. He wanted to see who owned the land next to his property. He tried to sound charming on the phone, but the woman sounded lethargic and proved somewhat uncooperative. She agreed to look into who owned the property, and she promised to call him back by the end of the week. But that wasn't fast enough. He tried his best to pressure her into doing it quicker, pleaded with her actually, but she didn't budge. She said this kind of inquiry took time, especially if it was a federal preserve or privately owned land trust. She hung up, and the line went dead.

Charles tried not to let the conversation deter him, so he decided to keep himself busy instead. He began unpacking a crate of collection bags and taps. Then, he spread the items out on the counter and scrutinized each one. He did this for close to an hour, humming along to classic rock songs on the radio. It was when he began slipping the items into a backpack, his true intentions became clear.

Charles had always been an honest man, but he was very lonely. The thought of marriage and children had kept him motivated for years, had even propelled him to establish his own business. But since he hadn't met that special someone yet, and hadn't even been on a date in years, his dreams gradually faded and died. He wanted more than anything to settle down and have a family, to teach his children how to play football or ride a bike or go fishing.

Unfortunately, lonely outings to bars yielded no results, and as the years went by, he grew accustomed to the fact that the fairer sex didn't want him. Then he gave up entirely and spent all of his evenings at home, cooking cheap TV dinners and watching late-night TV. He sold his house in town and moved into his hunting cabin full-time, far away from everything and everyone. But his heart ached.

And now, the thought of breaking onto someone's land didn't sit right with him. His stomach churned and flipped in cartwheels. He felt sick.

Eventually, he calmed himself down and pushed his troubling thoughts out of his mind. He needed to stay busy to keep his mind from wandering.

He collected up his gear and tools and slipped everything into his backpack, then trotted outside and gassed up his four-wheeler, connecting the trailer holding a forty-gallon collection barrel to the hitch. And then he was on his way.

Charles parked in the bushes and crept up to the fence. With a metal pry bar in hand, he sunk the end into the board and pried until he heard wood splinter. The nails retaliated in loud shrieks, and the board fell to the ground. He pried another board loose, then set his crowbar down and slipped through the opening.

4

He walked cautiously through the woods, inhaling the fresh scent of grass and maple trees. The sun was beginning to rise, and its brilliance shot through the branches in poetic flickers. He felt like he was entering another world. All his troubles seemed to melt away. Nature often did that to him.

Charles began his typical routine; he used his drill on the nearest tree and drilled down two inches, then hammered the tap into the wood as quietly as possible. He set up the collection bag, and no sooner had he put his drill back in his holder, he heard the familiar tree-speak clicking in that secret language he loved so much.

His heart soared.

He had always called it tree-speak, but it was just the sunlight warming up the sap and causing it to drip into the collection bags. He liked to pretend it was a language, nonetheless. He clicked back at the tree, trying to mimic the sound as closely as possible, then patted the bark and mouthed a quick prayer.

He tapped more trees. And to his surprise, the same thing happened with each one.

With a lighter heart, he made his way deeper into the property. He drilled more holes into more trees and collected more sap. And the whole time, he felt like a million dollars. It looked like his business would be saved after all.

After an hour, Charles grew weary. He sat down on a boulder to catch his breath and massage his aching feet. Once he got back to his four-wheeler, he'd empty the bags into the collection tank and return for more. If he could do this for the entire day, he would have something to show for his time. Even better, if he could do this for the next couple of days, his stock would be filled.

Charles gave a big stretch and was about to rummage around in his pack for another bag when he stopped himself short. He could have sworn the fence was south, just a couple hundred yards away. But it was nowhere to be seen. He couldn't even see any of the collection bags anymore. Did he get turned around?

He had grown up in the woods, hunting and fishing with his father, and he knew his way around the outdoors quite well. The fact that he had become lost confused him, especially with a fence as large as the Great Wall of China surrounding him.

He checked the sun and the moss growing on the trees and found his sense of direction, then headed south toward the creek, toward the spot he had entered. He walked for close to ten minutes and soon realized he had no clue where he was heading. It seemed like all four directions were suddenly askew. Nothing seemed right.

Then he heard it—a lonely female voice echoing through the woods.

The voice sounded high and sweet and reminded him of wind and honey. He closed his eyes and tried to pinpoint the source of the strange song. And the more he listened, the more it sounded like a *Kulning*, one of those beautifully eerie Scandinavian herding calls. Maybe he had wandered into a local pasture and was listening to a farmer calling her herd back home.

Then the voice stopped singing.

Inexplicable fear gripped his chest. He dropped his gear and ran as fast as he could, searching through the thickets and trees, trying to find the source of the haunting song. He thrashed through the bushes and tripped into a small clearing.

A young woman lay sprawled on the ground, hands propped under her chin. She had high cheekbones and golden hair, and she was nearly naked in a dress made of thistle and flowers that barely covered her breasts and thighs. She was so gorgeous he could hardly breathe. A circle of black stones surrounded her in the clearing. The dark rocks were as big as a fist and shimmered from the sun, reminding him of volcanic glass he had once seen in a museum.

She sang again. Time distorted, and everything shifted.

6

He found himself inside the circle of stones. She gazed deep into his eyes. Her own eyes were brilliant blue with flecks of hazel, and they reminded him of the reflection of fireworks in calm ocean water.

The woman opened her hand and held a seed in her palm. Lifting it to his mouth, she inserted it onto his tongue and then kissed him lightly until he swallowed it down. Her lips were soft and reminded him of a butterfly hopping from flower to flower and barely making a ripple in the flow of time. Then she kissed him again, deeper this time, and he yielded everything to her. He gave in.

A strange sensation clenched in his stomach and rose fiercely, biting at his temples. He felt scared and excited all at once. He tried to fight it down, to control his shaking arms, but it proved pointless. The strange woman had total control over him.

She draped her arms around his neck and drew him to the ground. She straddled him, her breasts heaving against his chest, her smooth thighs clamped around him like a vice. Her weight was both smothering and delicious. He never felt more alive.

She kissed him again. This time her tongue slid into his mouth and reminded him of a bee collecting nectar from a flower. He felt his whole body rise and sink slowly back into the ground, lost in an ocean of sand and time. He became trapped. But he didn't care. He had never experienced anything so sweet in all his life.

Then his heart fluttered and beat faster. His body stiffened, and he found he couldn't move a muscle.

From the pit of his stomach, he could feel the seed grow. It spread like an uncoiling snake, growing through his bowels and stomach, stretching into his esophagus, choking him, tearing through flesh, eviscerating his insides. He cried out in pain but found he couldn't pronounce any words.

The bones in his feet exploded through his boots. His toes stretched into knotted roots, tunneling deep into the soil, slicing through the dirt, seeking nourishment in the fertile spring soil. His skin became as thick as bark, and his arms grew into spindly branches. Finally, his eyes glossed over, but he could still see. He could sense everything moving around him in flickers.

Then the woman stood and walked away, leaving him to suffer alone in his new form. He tried to scream for her to stop, for her not to leave him, but his voice only echoed in his mind.

Time flowed, and she eventually returned with two young girls. They were about ten years old and just as beautiful as the woman, with long blonde hair and dresses made of ivy leaves. One child held a spigot and a bucket full of wooden tools. The other child cradled an empty basket and began picking up the black marker stones.

The girl with the spigot drew closer to him. She walked around him a few times and touched his body, rustling his foliage in approval. Then she placed the tip of the spigot on one of his arteries, and with the wooden mallet in hand, she pounded. Pain erupted through his core, followed by the sound of blood sloshing inside the bucket.

The girl stuck her finger inside the bucket and licked off the blood. The other child joined her in the tasting, and they both gave approving smiles. Finally, the mother joined, and they sat down in the clearing. They took turns dipping a wooden ladle into the bucket and sipping his maple blood.

And farther back in the soundscape, scattered amongst the wind and the woodland animals, the other trees whispered to him. It wasn't like before, when he had pretended to hear the trees talking; it was real this time.

The trees told him their own stories, of how they had wandered onto the property and become trapped, just like him. The trees talked about the ancient wood nymphs, how they were close to extinction in Northern Europe, and how they were transported across the sea and left to flourish unchecked in the preserve for hundreds of years.

But Charles didn't care about their ramblings. He didn't even care about his own physical pain. He now had a family who loved and depended upon him. He figured he had a good fifty years before he would mature enough to produce seeds of his own. He could wait that long.

Because to Charles, this wasn't enslavement. It was a chance at a new life.

And this warmed his lonely heart.

AUTHOR BIO

Aric Sundquist is an author of speculative fiction and the owner and editor of Dark Peninsula Press. Born and raised in Michigan's Upper Peninsula, he graduated from Northern Michigan University with a master's degree in Creative Writing. His short stories have appeared in numerous publications, including *The Best of Dark Moon Digest, Night Terrors III, Daylight Dims, Fearful Fathoms Vol* 1, and *Attic Toys.* A writer and a musician at heart, he also enjoys board games, guitar, and traveling. Currently, he lives in Marquette, Michigan, with his girlfriend and a ferocious beagle. You can visit his author website at: AricSundquist.weebly.com

THE FAERIE RING

BY LILLA GLASS

I was a young boy for most of my years—eight and one quarter, to be precise—and I was, quite frankly, bad at it. The lastborn of four and unusually feeble, I was tormented daily by my elder brothers. I couldn't count the times they spit in my porridge, hid newts in my boots, or used me as a slingshot target. Mother might well have ended their antics, but I'd never have tattled. My brothers were rascals through and through, but still, they were my heroes.

One morning, my eldest brother, Belmen, suggested we play hide-and-seek in the woods behind the farmhouse. Jemmy and Corwin were quick to agree. So naturally, I went along with it. Truth told; I was just excited they'd included me.

When Belmen began counting backward, I sprinted as far and fast as I could without a glance over my shoulder. Half a mile from the house, I found a hollow log to hide within. When thirty minutes ticked past, and I remained unfound, I began to feel quite clever. When an hour passed, I realized I'd been played for a fool.

Wiping blurry eyes, I crawled out from the hollow, determined to

11

prove I didn't need the others. I spent the whole afternoon turning the woods into my kingdom, crafting a castle of fallen branches, and whittling a sword from splintered oak. When a band of invisible marauders beset my keep, I protected it with the unwavering gallantry of a hero-king....at least, until my sword-arm tired. At that point, I politely asked the marauders to leave, and—being quite reasonable fellows beneath all that armor and war paint—they agreed.

The peasants showered me with accolades. They threw a feast in my honor and sang ballads of my victory. They wreathed my hair with a holly crown and wrote my name in the histories beside Sir Valance, Saint Callum, and Katermile the Bold.

But in the end, none of it mattered. Their songs were only of the robins, their food tasted of dust motes, and, when the realm's fairest maiden offered me a kiss, I could not feel her lips against my cheek.

Disillusioned, I abandoned my fortress. It was only kindling and my friends, mere daydreams. Try as I might, I could not convince myself otherwise.

I wandered the woods for a while after, my sword repurposed as a walking stick. Golden rays cut through the canopy, coaxing moss blossoms to life, and damselflies darted through the fiddleheads, their topaz bodies shimmering against the green. Yet, I could not appreciate the beauty of these simple things; I knew them too well, and they knew me too little. I might well have moped forever had I not stumbled upon something *new*.

The circle of toadstools, rigid and even as standing stones, stood the center of a lea dotted with buttercups and forget-me-nots. Sunlight poured heavily on their caps, but they cast no shadow. Compelled forward, I poked at the circle with the tip of my makeshift sword.

Nothing happened.

My mother had spoken of faerie rings. She'd said that, depending on the weight of the wind, they were as likely to bestow a curse as they were to grant a wish. My brothers had claimed her stories were nonsense, but my heart was younger and softer than theirs. My mind held more questions than doubts, and my veins, more wishes than blood.

Whether by instinct or enchantment, I somehow knew to pluck a handful of flowers before stepping into the circle. There, I closed my eyes, clutching the blossoms in one hand and my sword in the other, and I spoke the first words that came to mind.

"I wish I belonged somewhere."

Gravity lurched.

As I stumbled to the ground, my weapon and flowers fell free, and I covered my head. A second later, the world stopped shaking. I forced my eyes open. Familiar flowers smiled at me from outside the toadstool circle, and a deep disappointment flooded my chest. Heartbroken, I curled up in the center of the supposed faerie ring and wept, grateful that my brothers were not present to mock me for it.

"Are you alright?"

The voice was lullaby-soft and sunrise-bright, but it might as well have been a roar. I jolted to my knees, wiping my eyes clear as I twisted to face the speaker.

The woman was taller than any I'd seen before—though, admittedly, I'd not seen many—and dramatically more slender. Her skin was dark as oak bark, and her hair and eyes, golden as millet. She wore a seamless scarlet dress, buttoned in brass, and matching garnets glittered from her long, tapered ears.

"What are you?" I asked.

Her nose scrunched, and I realized the rudeness of my question. When she next spoke, her voice was richer than that which had roused me.

"We could ask you the same."

"W-we?"

In answer, a second burnished face peeked out from behind her waist.

13

This girl might have been my age, given her height (or lack thereof). When her eyes met mine, she giggled, hopping out from behind her living shield.

"I'm Midrianne!" she said, bouncing lightly on her slippered toes and offering a hand. "But people call me Midri!"

"I'm Arvis." I clasped her hand and let her pull me to my feet, and then I turned my attention to the woman. "And who are you?"

"Irrelevant," she replied, her scowl deepening.

"Actually, her name's Veila." Midri toyed with the pink ribbon that wound through her flaxen hair. "She's my sister, my watcher, and a helpless spoil-sport!"

Veila sighed, her golden eyes rolling. "Guilty on all counts. Someone has to keep you from trouble."

Midri cupped a hand around her mouth, whispering. "By 'trouble,' she means 'fun.'"

I chuckled half-heartedly; my mind bogged down with questions. "How did you get here?" I asked. "Did I somehow summon you?"

Veila and Midri exchanged puzzled glances.

"So, this *wasn't* Midri's doing?" said the elder. "How peculiar."

"I *told* you it wasn't!" Midri huffed, stamping her foot. "You never believe me!"

Veila ignored the outburst, kneeling to inspect the faerie ring. She plucked my fallen flowers from the ground—their petals now withered and their stalks dried brown. "Arvis, was it?"

"Yes."

"Well, Arvis, to answer your question, we walked here. How *you* got here is a much more pressing matter."

That didn't add up. If these girls lived near enough to walk to the family property, I'd surely have noticed them before.

"I *live* here!" I said, turning to point toward the farmhouse. "Right over...."

This was not the forest I knew.

Beyond the familiar wildflower lea lay a tangle of foreign green, brimming with peculiar blossoms. In the distance, gilded spires rose above the canopy, stretching wistfully towards a cloudless, cerulean sky. Luminous dots—like fireflies, only brighter—swirled on the winds like effervescent eddies. As they swept past, I could swear I heard them *giggling*.

My skin prickled—not with fear, but with excitement. "Where am I?"

"No more free answers!" Midri raced around the toadstools to face me. "You tell me *what* you are, and I'll tell you *where*."

"I already told you, I'm Arvis!"

Midri shook her head. "That's *who,* not *what*! Let's see.... You're ghostly pale, but the sunlight isn't hurting you. Not Unseelie, then...." She snapped her fingers, smiling brightly. "You're a mortal, aren't you? I've read of your kind in storybooks, but I never thought I'd see one for real!" Her eyes flitted to her sister, her fingers folding in a plea. "Can we keep him, Veila? Pretty pleeease?"

"Absolutely not!" said Veila. "Remember what happened to that pet hazel witch you begged for? Or the phoenix? Or the fawn? Our garden has no more room for graves, Midri!"

"But I'll take good care of him, promise! He probably eats less than a fawn and needs less space than a phoenix. And I won't forget to water him either; he's cuter than the hazel witch was!"

No one had ever called me *cute* before. "I'm a person," I muttered, my face flushing warm. "Not a pet!"

Midri pouted. "That's exactly what the hazel witch said."

"This has certainly been interesting," Veila said from behind me. "But it's past time for Arvis here to head back home."

"But I only just got here!" I hurried out of the circle to hide behind Midri. At that moment, I'd have rather been a faerie's pet than the family

15

runt—even if she occasionally forgot to feed me. "I'll be good, I promise! I.... I'm toilet trained and everything!"

Even Veila chuckled at that one, though not for long. "I don't think you understand your situation," she said, straightening to her full, imposing height. "Every second you spend here has a price, and too many will cost your life."

To a child, nothing is more valuable than the immediate. "I'll worry about that when it happens."

"My thoughts exactly!" Midri said.

Veila rubbed her temple, sighing. "You two were cut from the same cloth, weren't you?"

"Cotton." Midri looked to me for confirmation. "Lace is too itchy, and velvet's too clingy."

"Um.... sure."

Midri seemed happy enough with the answer. "So, we can keep him, then?" she asked Veila. "You wouldn't rip a nice garment in half, would you?"

Veila ignored her sister, circling the ring. She paused beside a couple of crushed mushrooms, prodding them with her foot. "You broke it," she said, pensive. "That's.... inconvenient."

"I'm *so* sorry," I lied. "I suppose I'll have to wait until they regrow."

"Yes," Veila grinned. "Good thing that will only take a moment, with the right tincture, and I happen to have some at home. You'll just have to stay here while we retrieve it." She started toward the treeline, motioning for Midri to follow.

The younger sister didn't budge. "He should come with!" she said.

Veila paused. "That thing is not following us home!"

"I'll stay with him, then." Midri played with the hem of her white dress. "Can't guarantee we'll be here when you return."

Veila's response was something halfway between a groan and a growl. "Fine then," she said. "Just keep your pace up."

When she resumed her march, I started swiftly after her, excited to see more of the vivid world. After only a few steps, Midri caught my sleeve.

"Don't forget your sword!" she said, nodding toward the branch I'd abandoned. "You never know when you'll need it!"

I shrugged, pulling my arm free. "It's just a stick."

"Fine," Midri smirked. "Don't say I didn't warn you."

Our walk took roughly twenty minutes, and I savored every splendid second of it. At first, I stuck close to Midri as she skipped and darted through the forest. Curious eyes blinked out from the shadows as we climbed half-felled trees, swung from flowering vines, and used giant agates as stepping-stones to traverse silvery streams. She showed me many a wonderous sight along the way—flocks of songbirds with feathers bright as a sunrise, fuchsia berries that made sugar lumps seem bitter, and tiny pixies perched on thrones of lily and orchid, their translucent wings aglow. But Midri's energy was boundless, and I was only a mortal. When I could no longer keep up with her, I returned to the trail, falling into step behind Veila.

"Your home is lovely," I said, trying to make conversation. "Do others live here?"

"There are others in this valley," she said curtly, her gaze locked on the path ahead. "But we are alone with our echoes."

The conversation dropped right there, and I didn't dare pick it back up.

Eventually, the foliage thinned, and a stunning building came into view. It dwarfed my family's farmhouse in both height and girth, and I thought it might be a palace, though it lacked the traditional drawbridge and battlements. Gilded pillars surrounded the bottom floor, branching like elms as they climbed to the second story, where they transformed into a glimmering filigree balcony. As I stepped from the woods, I craned my neck, following the rooftop to where it seemed to meet the sky. The shingles flared like sun-washed pyrite, nearly blinding in their brilliance.

"You live here?" I asked, stunned.

No one answered.

Veila was already ten feet off, climbing the front steps. I rushed after her, but Midri jumped out from the underbrush, barring my path.

"En garde!" she shouted, poking me in the side with a slender stick.

"What?"

"You're dead!" She poked me a second time. "I tried telling you to carry a weapon!"

"Oh, no!" I gasped, fighting a smile as I tumbled backward to the ground. I held my breath, closing my eyes and letting my tongue loll out of my mouth.

Midri giggled for some time after; it was tough to wait her out.

"Oh, knock it off, Arvis!" she said once her laughter finally faded. "It's not even a real sword!"

When I didn't reply, I heard a branch drop to the path, followed by the hurried patter of slippered feet.

"You're jesting, surely!" Midri said, her voice frantic as she jostled my arm. "Oh, Veila will be furious if we have to bury another!"

Carefully as I could manage, I felt through the ferns until my fingers brushed a decently sized stick. Before Midri could notice, I tapped it against her side.

"Hey!" She hopped backward with another bout of giggles. "You were *supposed* to be dead!"

"And now you are!" I scrambled to my feet; makeshift weapon raised.

Midri plucked her fallen sword from the soil, pointing it toward me. "Face me on fair terms, Unseelie scum!"

I had no idea what *Unseelie* meant, but Midri looked equally confused when I shouted, "My pleasure, marauder!" so I supposed *Unseelies* and *Marauders* were similar things. I lunged forward, my sword

18

slicing through the air, and she swiftly parried my attack. I pivoted away, dodging the blow. When I knelt to sweep her ankles, she leapt over the branch, and, upon landing, she slammed her weapon down upon mine. The impact made my fingers tremble, and I nearly lost my grip.

"Had enough, fiend?" she asked.

"Not nearly," I replied, diving back into battle.

I had been in dozens of play swordfights, all weighted too heavily in my favor. It was different, facing a true foe—a true *friend*. Whenever Midri's weapon struck my own, joy sparked in my soul, comfortable and warm. By her smile, she felt the same. We did not lay down our arms until the bark had chipped away from our branches, leaving them nearly bare.

"I won," Midri declared proudly as her sword dropped back to the dirt.

"Did not," I said.

"Did so."

"Did not!"

"Did so!"

"Doesn't matter." I smiled, settling on the grass to catch my breath. "The game itself was the point of it."

Midri sat cross-legged beside me, smirking, and I was glad the play-fight hadn't turned to a real one.

"You have a lovely home," I said, nodding toward the giant house.

"I suppose." Midri shifted uncomfortably. "It feels empty ever since...."

I didn't need to ask the question to know the answer. I didn't like talking about my late father either, not even to my brothers.

"I'm so sorry," I said instead.

Midri shrugged, brightening suddenly. "It's not so bad. They'll be reborn. In the meantime, I have Veila. And now I have you!"

At that moment, Veila emerged from the house, a bottle of glowing green liquid cradled in one arm. "Took me a while to find it," she said, drifting down the steps. "But, now that I have, it's time to go."

Midri latched onto my arm, squeezing tightly. "But.... but we're friends now."

Veila shook her head. "That's why you shouldn't take strays home, Midri. Surely, his family misses him."

I wasn't so sure, but given the conversation I'd just had with Midri, it would have been calloused to say so.

"I don't want to leave," I said instead. Regardless of how my family felt, Midri was my friend—my first one—and Veila had potential. Already, she'd paid me more attention than my brothers ever had. "I don't belong there."

"You don't belong here either."

The words made me wince. "But I *must*," I said. "That's what I wished for in the faerie ring: somewhere to belong."

"The rings are only gateways, Arvis." Veila's hand was warm on my shoulder, her voice sympathetic. "They don't grant wishes."

Midri kept her grip on my arm, her sniffles echoing my own, as her elder sister coaxed us to our feet and guided us down the forest path. That second trip ought to have been as enchanting as the first, no matter how my tears blurred my vision, but sorrow had seeped into my spirit, and it darkened the scenery a little more with every somber step.

Before I knew it, we'd arrived back at the faerie ring. Numbly, I watched as Veila poured her tincture onto the crushed toadstools. Perhaps I might have run, but my heart was too heavy and my legs too leaden. It took a few minutes for the toadstools to resurrect. Midri spoke the whole time, her voice a solemn song. I forget the lyrics.

After shepherding me to the center of the circle, Veila shoved a wildflower bouquet into one of my hands— "for the ease of leaving," she said—and a handful of brittle bark chips into the other, "for the agony of arriving."

20

I might have asked about that second part had I been more lucid.

"What am I supposed to wish for?" I asked absently.

"I don't think the words matter so much as your faith," Veila answered. "Whatever you ask, you need to mean it."

I could not fathom a longing half as strong as that which had brought me there, but I nodded anyway. I waved at Midri, mouthing a goodbye before closing my eyes and reciting the only wish I could think of at the time. "I wish to find my way back here, someday."

For the second time that day, the world shook. A heartbeat later, a white-hot pain burned through my bones, sending me toppling to the earth. My skin turned to fire and my organs to ice, and needle-sharp pains raced up and down my spine. Time lost meaning as I flailed against the grass, consumed by utter anguish, my wails echoing through a pitch-dark night.

Then I recalled Veila's second offering. Taking a wild guess, I shoved the bark chips into my mouth. My trembling fingers had crushed them to bits, and my sweat had soaked them soggy, but sharp splinters still lodged in my gums as I gnashed, adding bitter brine to the tastes of dirt and daylight. The moment I swallowed, the pain began receding, a tingling numbness biting at its heels. I curled inward, gasping for air, and my throat prickled dully with every eager breath.

"Are you alright?"

The voice didn't belong to Midri, but the question brought to mind her bubbling laughter and her sister's gleaming eyes. Thinking back on those pleasant things, I let the darkness take me.

I awoke to the mixed aromas of boiled cabbage and cinnamon tea. A heavy quilt had been draped over my aching body and a rag over my forehead. Both were soaked in sweat.

A man slept in the chair beside me. His face was hauntingly familiar. I stared at him for a long time, transfixed by the subtle creases in the corners of his eyes, before I could convince myself of his identity. Though time had carved his round face to angles and years of toil had broadened his slender shoulders, I'd have recognized that head of dark curls—so like our father's—anywhere, not to mention the mocking smirk that graced his lips even while he slumbered.

"Belmen?" I asked, my voice gravel.

His lashes flickered, but he didn't wake.

Indeed, his age was an omen. I sat up, gritting my teeth to keep from crying out as agony sang through my skeleton. Sure enough, my bare feet poked out from the end of a quilt that would have drowned me hours before. I lifted a hand, marveling at its size and at the bruises that blossomed at every joint. That morning, I had been a little boy. I wasn't a little boy anymore, and it didn't bother me in the least.

"You're awake."

My head snapped toward the voice, and my neck ached bitterly for it.

Belmen's eyes were kinder than they'd ever been, shimmering with concern. "It's really you, isn't it, Arvis?" he asked.

"Yes," I rasped.

The fissures in his face deepened. "I'm so sorry, brother. I never thought I'd have the chance to say it, but—" His voice snapped like chalk, and he set a calloused hand atop my own. "What happened to you? Where did you go?"

I didn't know how to answer, so I didn't.

The door creaked—a welcome interruption—and a stranger peeked into the room. Her hair was a mess of dark curls, glossy as varnished maple, and her eyes glittered green in the lamplight. Perhaps, that morning, I'd have thought her pretty. I wondered if I'd ever find beauty in any earthly thing again.

"Supper's ready," the woman said to Belmen. "And your other brothers have arrived."

22

He rose, and I followed him into the dining room, where Jemmy and Corwin greeted me with wide, teary smiles. A pot of cabbage stew sat at the center of the table. It didn't smell like Mother's.

My head was elsewhere for most of that supper, but I learned a lot in my more attentive moments. I'd vanished a decade before. A few years after, Mother passed away from the yellow cough, leaving the farm to Belmen and his wife. Jemmy and Corwin were working in town now, both for different blacksmiths.

The conversation circled like a buzzard for a long while until Jemmy asked the same question Belmen had—the one they'd all been wondering about: "What happened to you, Arvis?"

I still couldn't think of a good answer, so I told the truth—all of it. I told them of the faerie ring and my wish, then I told them about Veila and Midri. I spoke of the magical, colorful world beyond the ring—the rapture of seeing and tasting it, the despair of leaving it behind. At the end of my tale, they all looked askance, disbelieving.

"I'm sure it's been difficult." Belmen placed his hand on my shoulder. "In time, your memories will clear up."

Time passed, but my memories did not waver. I clung to them like ivy to bricks. Belmen was either kind or remorseful enough to let me stay at the farmhouse until I found my footing. I suppose I never quite found it. His wife thought me simple; I overheard her whispering to my brother about my peculiar ways. She thought it strange, the way I'd wander off into the woods at night, nary an explanation.

I'd crushed the faerie ring upon my return—flailed overtop it until there was nothing left but a dark patch of dirt. I tried everything I could think of to coax it back to life. I even plucked other toadstools from throughout the woods, planting them in the circle where the others had stood. No luck. Eventually, I began to believe it had never really been there, as my brothers claimed. That I'd suffered something tragic, and my mind made up a happier tale.

But my dreams—oh, those were vivid things, rife with adventure and piskies and glittering tawny eyes. *Those* remained brilliant, even after a year had passed, and I was still living off my brother's pity, waiting for toadstools to sprout in a muddy circle.

By then, my mind had just about caught up with my body, and I decided to go out and make a life for myself, however meager. I found work at a nearby mill, and the owner allowed me to sleep in a shack on the property's edge. Most of my days were spent in a haze—the light was too dull, the food too bland, the music too flat, and the smiles too cold—but I worked hard enough to earn my keep.

I made a better man than a boy. At the very least, I looked the part. After a few months of labor, my shoulders were broader than my brothers', my arms were thicker, and my chin, prouder. Many local girls gave me their attention, a few gave me kisses, and one—Kela—gave me her heart. That's what her letter had said, anyway. Within weeks, she took it back, claiming I was too distant and broken a person.

That same night, I decided to visit Belmen. Well, not *him* so much as the family property. As I hiked through those woods, I felt certain that my mind had snapped, but I also knew my heart would wither unless I made my wish one final time. I held my breath, stepping into that moonlit clearing, only to lose it when my eyes landed on a miraculous ring of moonlit toadstools. Unthinking, I tore a handful of flowers from the grass and hopped into the circle, muttering the exact words I'd uttered at age eight.

I was prepared for the sudden lurch, but it still knocked me to my knees. I gasped upon landing, and a warm, honeyed wind swept through my soul, stirring it from a long and restless slumber. A sudden brilliance nearly blinded me, so I raised my hand as a shield.

A shrill squeal pierced the air, startling me. I jumped, dropping my hand, and spinning toward the sound. Not five feet away stood a beautiful woman, clothed in red and brass. A trembling child peeked out from behind her, eying me uncertainly.

"Wh-who are you?" the girl asked.

Honestly, the question was offensive—I'd recognized them both in the span of a blink—but I supposed I couldn't blame her, given the circumstances.

"You don't remember me?" I asked, smiling so wide it hurt.

Neither sister had changed a bit since we met, though my perception of them had undoubtedly shifted. Midri was the tiniest thing; standing stick-straight, she hardly hit my elbow. Veila was poised as proudly as ever, but she could no longer look down on me. I could read her expression better from this angle, and it was softer than I remembered it.

"You can't be Arvis!" Midri said, slipping into the open and taking a timid step toward me. She looked up at her sister. "It can't be, right? He's not near as cute as before!"

Veila blushed brightly, making me think—or perhaps hope—she disagreed. "It's Arvis alright," she said, her voice a half-sigh. "I suppose this means I owe you five coppers."

"I knew it!" Midri lit up like a firefly, bolting forward and wrapping her spindly arms around my waist, nearly tackling me to the grass. "I just knew it would work!"

I laughed, ruffling her hair. "You knew *what* would work?"

Veila smirked, crossing her arms. "You were so adamant that you'd *wished* yourself here that you convinced Midri such things were possible. She's been hopping in and out of that circle for hours now, trying to wish you back."

"And it worked!" Midri released me, skipping over to her sister. "I can keep him now, right?"

I chuckled. "I'm not a pet!"

"Of course, you're not," Veila agreed, turning to walk toward the tree-line. "But you *are* a bit of a stray, aren't you? I suppose no one could stop you from following us home."

"You're not going to make me go back to where I came from?" I asked.

"Now, why would I do that?" Veila smiled over her shoulder. "You belong here."

AUTHOR BIO

Lilla Glass is an author from Olympia, WA. While fantasy is her first love, she dabbles in horror, sci-fi, and the occasional (gasp!) non-speculative work. In winter 2021, she signed a four-book deal with City Owl Press for her darkly whimsical high fantasy series, *The Reel of Rhysia*. The first installment, *The Unseen*, is set to be released in July 2023. Lilla also has two short stories being published in fall 2021 by Thaw for Mystic Owl Press and Fresh Game for Papillon du Père Publishing. For more information, please visit Lilla online at LillaGlass.com

THE DRIVE

BY VICTOR NANDI

"Hello!"

Parisa turned her head to see who had spoken. She discovered a bald, middle-aged man of plump build wearing a grey suit.

"I'm Rufus," he beamed, his manners overkeen.

And I am the co-passenger that wishes to be left alone; Parisa's face reflected her thought.   "Parisa," she uttered. Her sea-green eyes showed little warmth as she spoke.

Parisa sat in a two-person seat, which up until that moment she had enjoyed in solitude.

"Ah!" Rufus plopped himself into the aisle seat beside Parisa and typed in his phone. "Is that one 's' or two?" he asked.

Parisa didn't reply, but Rufus found what he'd been searching for.

"A fairy?" he said, his tone flattering. "Like an angel?"

"I assure you," she turned her gaze towards the small window she sat beside. "I am not."

"So, what are you?" he asked, eyeing her toned legs.

Parisa scowled.

28

"I mean, what's your field?" Rufus said, his tone defensive. "Where do you work?"

"Lifeguard Mutual....I'm in sales."

All the tourists had taken their seats, and nearby a clock struck three o'clock in the morning. Sunrise Point was just a couple of hours away. The bus's engine roared to life.

"Three hundred dollars a month, and the insurance covers *all* forms of illness?"

Parisa turned away again. Rufus had his phone in his hand, and he was scrolling through the Lifeguard Mutual website.

"Yes," she tried to smile professionally but couldn't.

"Like from a common cold to cancer?"

"Yes," she looked outside the window.

Rufus studied her dark hair, sharp-cut face, and curves. He seemed more than pleased in her apparel, a casual, orange mini skirt.

"I," he cleared his throat, "err... I like it." He goggled at her breasts, and Parisa wished she'd worn a bra that day.

"Submit your contact information, and when I return to work, I will email you a copy of the contract," Parisa cursed herself for disclosing to him the name of her employer.

"I wish we could complete it now," he said.

Parisa didn't reply.

"Maybe you could email it from your phone?" he hesitated. "Only if you want to, of course."

Reluctantly, she pulled her phone out.

"Great!" Rufus was elated. "I'll just go through the contract on the way, then."

The empty road snaked around the mountainside, and the bus picked up the pace.

Parisa scrolled through her phone, the wind raking through her hair. She felt Rufus's eyes wander down her flapping neckline.

Parisa tapped on a file and handed her phone to Rufus.

"Un-fucking-believable!" exclaimed a ginger-haired stranger from the back seat.

"Make sure you go through everything in there," Parisa said, not wanting to be disturbed for a while. "Be sure to check it twice."

"Certainly," Rufus said, still leering at her neckline.

"Fifteen minutes into a vacation, and already gouging other passengers for business," the ginger-haired fellow from the back seat shouted. "Woman, why do you even *live* on this planet?"

The insulting remark was loud enough to draw attention.

"Wait for a couple more years, and I'll be selling insurance on the moon," Parisa, unabashed, yelled back.

The retort drew a stifling wave of laughter from the other passengers.

"What about the monsters?" asked a curious, little boy curled up next to his mother.

Parisa considered ignoring the boy but realized too many faces were looking at her, waiting for her response.

"Monsters?"

"The ones that live on the moon?" the boy exclaimed, "My mom says they're terrifying."

That's because your mom is a moron, Parisa thought, grinning. "In that case, I won't sell insurance on the moon," she shrugged, "It's not for monsters anyway."

"You think that's funny, huh?" a grave voice said.

Everybody in the cabin turned to see who spoke. It was a fragile man, possibly in his mid-fifties, with messy, brown hair and a brooding face. He wore a blue, cotton shirt and white, tweed trousers.

Parisa sighed. It felt like the entire bus had conspired against allowing her some quiet time.

30

"I didn't mean to offend you, sir," she forced the words out. "I was just stating the obvious."

"And what's that?" the brooding man stared hard at her.

Parisa paused for a moment, deciding whether to speak her candid thoughts or keep quiet. "Colonization begins with clearing the land of monsters," she spoke slowly. "This has always been the way on Earth, and the same thing will happen when we move *beyond* Earth."

"And you think that's ethical?"

"It doesn't matter what I think," Parisa looked out the window. Outside, it had begun to drizzle. "It's just the way things are."

"Well, humans have had it their way for far too long," the brooding man said in an ominous tone. "Their due is right around the corner."

"If you say so," she waved her hand dismissively, then stretched it out of the window.

"You know who's going to give it to them?" he continued.

"Nope," the cold droplets on Parisa's palm felt so good. She needed an escape from the meaningless discussion that was piquing more and more attention from the other tourists.

"Monsters," the man said as if he was offering a revelation to everyone.

Parisa stared at him with disbelief, as did many others.

There was silence for a while, and then, some of the tourists bent over with laughter.

"And I took you for a serious man," Parisa didn't attempt to hide her disdain.

"He means it figuratively," said a young, blonde woman sitting in the front row. "Rapid industrialization, cutting down trees, global warming.... look around you. We have been destroying the earth to expand our civilization. Sooner or later, nature *will* retaliate. And when it does, it will be monstrous."

31

"You may be right about nature," the man grumbled, "But I was *very* literal with what I said."

No one laughed this time. It felt like a story was on the way. With Sunrise Point still far off, a story would be a pleasant means to kill boredom.

The drizzle became heavy rainfall, and people started closing the windows. Everybody *except* Parisa. She savored the raindrops on her skin. The cold water seemed to help her wash the frustration away.

"Do you think they made the Chimera for entertainment?" the old man continued, "Or created the Basilisk just for decorating their legends?"

"No, sir," Parisa sounded amused, "Those exist, I assure you."

"Yes, they do," he pounded on the seat, indifferent to the ridicule.

"Where?" asked a tall woman from the crowd.

He was about to answer, but just then, the bus pulled over.

"What happened?" someone asked.

The uniformed driver was an older man with a headful of silver hair and a furrowed face.

"I don't know," he peered through the windshield, "I don't remember seeing *two* roads here."

"*Remember!?*" the ginger-haired man from the backseat who had taunted Parisa earlier snapped, "How long has it been, old man?"

"Long enough," the driver replied.

"Where's the regular guy?"

"Down with flu."

"Now, isn't this just great?" the ginger-haired fellow scoffed, "Do you at least have GPS?"

"Won't work out here."

"Why?"

"You tell me."

People began to check their phones. It was true; nobody had coverage.

"Nothing gets past the hills around here," the driver said.

32

"What a fiasco!" an aged woman remarked.

"Which road do we take, then?" moaned a man with rabbit-like eyes.

"Let's vote," Parisa suggested.

"Are you fucking serious?" the ginger-haired guy barked.

"Worst case, we miss the sunrise and head back to base after an agreeable trip through the mountains," Parisa said, pointedly, "or we could just sit here all day."

"Don't mock me, woman," he glared at Parisa.

"Do you have a better suggestion?" the blonde woman at the front asked.

The ginger-haired guy paused for a moment, making up his mind, "We go that way," he stood up and pointed towards the road on the left. "How many of you agree?"

A few tourists raised their hands.

He turned to Parisa. "What about you?" His tone was derogatory.

"The other road, of course," Parisa shrugged at being asked the obvious.

He snickered, "And how many of you agree with the insurance salesman?"

Rufus raised his hand, along with a few others.

"So," the ginger-haired guy declared, "The vote is clear. We go left. Godspeed to-"

"Wait!" Rufus stood up.

Everyone stared at him.

"Sunrise Point is a popular tourist spot," Rufus moved to the front of the vehicle. "Do you think the road leading there would be so dark?"

"And yet here we are," the ginger-haired man pointed outside, "facing two roads, each one as dark as the other."

"Are you sure of that?" Rufus flicked the switches.

33

The lights inside the bus went out. It was a wagon of darkness swathed by the rainy night. Everybody looked out the windows, and at once, they all saw a speck of light flickering in the distance down the road to the right.

"He's right. We need to go right, towards the light," someone said, and everybody nodded.

Rufus flipped the lights back on, and people returned to their seats. The driver obediently turned towards the fork in the right of the road.

"If someone had noticed that sooner, it would have saved us some time," the ginger-haired fellow snapped.

"If the price to watch you lose is just a couple of minutes," countered Rufus, "I think the deal was worth it."

"Maybe you should sign that *guard your life* or whatever contract right away," the ginger-haired man stared coldly at Rufus, "because if you're wrong, you will need one hell of a life insurance policy."

"Is that a threat?" Rufus hissed.

"No. Just a warning. It's the rainy season up on these mountains. You could catch the flu, you know."

Fired up, Rufus opened his mouth to respond.

"Chill out," Parisa stopped him, "You have already made a scene. We're on the right path now."

Rufus looked at her, a twinkle in his eyes, "How do you know for sure this is the right path?"

"Well, your explanation seemed logical to me," she said, sounding a wee bit grateful.

At that moment, half a mile behind them, the forking on the road wobbled like a giant ripple upon still waters. The breeze changed its course, rather unnaturally, as if an invisible force was sucking the wind into a vortex. And then, the wobbling subsided, leaving behind a *single*, straight road. The fork in the path had disappeared.

"Coming back to our discussion," the blonde woman at the front

34

looked at the brooding man, "Where do monsters like the basilisk and the chimera exist?"

"And here they go again," Parisa whispered under her breath.

The pause at the fork in the road had lasted for a few minutes, at least, but still was not long enough for the passengers to forget their prior conversation.

"Yes!"

"Valid question."

"Yeah, where do they exist in the real world?"

Eagerness poured out of the passengers.

The brooding man, now on the spot, stared back at all of them, "Where else but in the crooked mind of man?"

Sounds of disappointment reverberated throughout the cabin.

"You're contradicting yourself, sir," said the man with rabbit-like eyes.

"Don't you get it?" the brooding man exclaimed, "Head of an animal, body of another, the tail of something else.... it's an idea crafted to arouse fear and stir up hate."

"And what exactly is to be gained by that?" questioned the aged woman.

"Power," he paused for dramatic effect. "Humans wanted *power* over beings they couldn't control. So, they made monsters of them, painted them with ugly, frightening colors, and fed misinformation to the people. Why do you think they sell the stories at the village squares and paint the basilicas with frightening images?"

"To spread a wrong idea," the ginger-haired man derided him in mock assent. "Totally worth the investment."

"Power is a powerful motivator, young man," he insisted, "and spreading wrong ideas is an age-old method to retain power. Do you want to know how hard it is to fight a false notion that's been sunken deep into

35

the minds of people?"

"So, if monsters, as we have heard of in stories, are false depictions," Rufus asked, "then what *is* the truth?"

Everybody turned their attention back to the brooding man. "The truth..." he said slowly, "is that they are *just like us.* They don't have shape-shifting bodies or heads of lions or tails of serpents. They are just like you and me, and they're hiding in back alleys and lurking behind dating profiles...."

".... prowling under beds," Parisa rolled her eyes and rose from her seat. She was beyond annoyed.

At once, Rufus's attention shifted. Parisa's loose hemline grazed her thighs. Shamelessly, he switched on his phone's video recorder and held the phone over his knee. Parisa tied her hair in a ponytail and moved past Rufus.

"Figuring out newer means," the man continued, "to take *just enough* to survive."

When she had strolled away, Rufus played the clip. Parisa's baggy casual wear had given away more than he had expected. She had nothing on under the dress. Rufus gaped at her naked butt.

Parisa walked over to the front, taking notice of Rufus ogling the video on his phone.

Pathetic, she thought.

Ignoring Rufus and the conversation, she went to stand behind the driver.

"So, how's it going?" she asked.

The driver didn't reply.

"How far are we from our destination?" Parisa tried again.

The man slowly turned his head towards her. His wrinkled face was pale and expressionless, and his eyes were frozen like the eyes of a dead man.

"Almost there," he said in a monotonous voice. "We are almost to

36

our destination."

Parisa looked outside. The concrete road had disappeared. As far as her eyes could see, dense forest surrounded them. Not a single human habitat was in sight, let alone Sunrise Point. Weirder, the trees had begun to shake, unstable images on a digital screen.

Behind her, Parisa heard Rufus tell the other passengers something was wrong, but the rest of the cabin was silent. Parisa turned to see all the other passengers sitting motionless as statues.

"What's going on?" Rufus stood up, alarmed.

Parisa glanced at the frozen tourists and said to the driver, "Stop the bus."

The driver slammed on the brakes.

"Hey, dude," Rufus shook the ginger-haired man by his shoulders. "You win; we went the wrong way." But the ginger-haired man didn't respond. He just sat unmoving, staring into an invisible void.

Parisa unlatched the front door and stepped into the pouring rain.

The surrounding forest glitched and disintegrated, and the grass faded out as if wiped clean with the quick strokes of a giant eraser.

Rufus ran out of the bus, "Hey!"

Parisa's gaze swept over the transforming surroundings. She didn't reply.

Parisa stood by the trunk of a dead tree. Rufus watched her; but with irritation, Parisa noted his eyes still wandered downwards to ogle at the wet garments that clung to her body.

"Those peo-people," Rufus stuttered, his eyes glued to the now see-through fabric of her blouse. "They aren't— "

He was interrupted as a bloodcurdling screech tore through the air. Parisa stepped aside, and Rufus's face drained of color.

"Get away," he said, as a slithering, green creature emerged into the misty dawn. It crept forward on four limbs, a sap-like slime running down its body. Its shape resembled that of a human, but palm-sized scales covered its body.

Rufus's pallor gained a green tinge.

The creature stared at Rufus with icy, green eyes. It snarled, and the stiff bristles on its head quivered.

Parisa stood, watching. Slowly, every trace of foliage vanished, leaving behind a forbidding landscape rutted with crannies that smoldered in the rain. The ground had rocky holes scattered around. The first light of day edged over the horizon, creating sparkles in the muddy puddles that surrounded them.

The creature screeched, and other creatures slowly crept out of the fissures and crawled towards the tour bus, their fangs dripping with anticipation.

"Parisa!" Rufus hurried to grab her hand. "We must go!" He stumbled over a dead root and fell on his stomach, nearly hitting his head on a rock.

The creatures swarmed the bus and pounced on the waiting prey. No cries of terror or wails of agony erupted from the frozen passengers. The night was filled with the sounds of blood splattering on the bus's windows, and the shredding of flesh, the ripping of organs, the crackling of bones and the munching of raw meat.

Rufus began to rise but stopped, scared stiff. A puddle on the ground had a reflection of one of the creatures, lapping its drooling fangs with its grey, forked tongue. The creature's scaly face glared at him with sea-green eyes.

Rufus looked up. Parisa stood there, her beautiful, scarlet tongue dancing in perfect sync with the reflection of the slimy creature.

AUTHOR BIO

Victor Nandi is a Lead Content Developer with an Ed-tech company. In addition to various international magazines and journals, his works of horror, fantasy, and sci-fi have featured in anthologies from several publication houses worldwide. When he isn't spending time with the characters from his imagination, he is usually chatting with friends and family about investment tools, sugar-free diets, and workout regimes. He can often be found curled up in his cave with a novel or trying to cheer up a dispirited friend with a horror story. He lives in Bangalore, India. Feel free to connect with him at: Instagram.com/Victor.Nandi_

THE WATCHER ON THE MOUNTAIN

BY CORY MASON

I worked the late shift because it suited me to be alone. Sitting at the front desk, "keeping watch" during the night, only interacting with the occasional bleary-eyed patron. True, the view of a dimly lit parking lot through a set of glass doors left a lot to be desired, but I was the only employee in the building. No micromanagement, no coercion to look like I'm constantly working. I was free to watch YouTube videos and sketch on motel notepads all night long. I could be alone.

I had this running project going. I would scratch out a few shapes on a notepad page and then tape it to a collection of similar doodled pages, adding a few each night. I almost had a three-by-two foot panoramic sketch of the front lobby from the vantage point of my desk. Not the most inspired work, sure, but I was getting pretty good.

Just before dawn, the head custodian, Rita, a tiny woman with ironworker's hands and blonde hair dulled to a muted platinum with age, slowly made her way through the front doors. The chilled desert air blew in with her. She didn't wave, and neither did I. We had a mutual understanding that neither of us was interested in interaction at this time of day. Rita needed her coffee, and I needed my comfortable distance from people.

I sighed to myself as Rita disappeared into the break room, and the whine of the ragged Mr. Coffee spun up like a lopsided jet engine. It wouldn't be long before more and more people started walking through those doors. The last couple of hours of my shift were always my least favorite part of the day. I sank further and further down into my chair, trying to disappear.

Josh Cox, the insufferable manager, pushed through the front doors around eight. Thankfully he gave me little acknowledgment beyond the disdainful glance that constituted a greeting between us. I was safe to wheedle away the last hours of my shift in relative peace.

When ten o'clock came, I punched my timecard, releasing myself back into the normal world. I turned and headed for the door as quickly as possible, keeping my head down. I was so close to free, so close to being away from all these people. But as I put my hand on the front door's push bar, I heard exactly the thing I didn't want to hear.

"Ed, I need you."

Not once had Josh Cox ever needed me. He had never given me any responsibility he didn't have to. He had never expected anything of me, except to sit at the desk and wait out the night, and only because *somebody* had to do it.

The only instances that I ever heard "Ed, I need you" were when Josh felt like dumping some stupid tasks on me that he wanted to do even less than he trusted me not to fuck it up. Plus, I think Josh needed to prove to himself sometimes that he could make me do whatever he wanted. "Various other duties as assigned" was a bullshit job description clause.

So, I turned around and approached my boss, working the painful hunch out of my shoulders and silently waiting for him to give me whatever unpleasant task he had in store.

Josh was tall and prematurely rounding at the edges. His metabolism must have betrayed him somewhere around age twenty-five, rolling him down toward a pear-shaped office body ever since. He carried his weight around his thighs in an unfortunate way that was difficult not to stare at, but staring was probably not a smart career move. But Josh was happy to stare at me, stretching the silence past the point of awkwardness, until finally deciding to speak.

He smacked a wad of spearmint-green gum while he spoke. "The guy in 121 didn't answer his wakeup call, and he just missed check-out. Go wake him up and get him out of there so the maids can do their jobs."

I wanted to tell him to piss off. I wanted to tell him that wasn't my job. I wanted to tell him my shift was over. There were a lot of things I wanted to say. But I didn't. It would be faster just to do the thing. Then I could be alone.

Without a word, I walked past Josh in the direction of the guest rooms to do what I was told. He scoffed as I went like I had somehow done something wrong by doing what he told me. I don't get people.

Once I was out of earshot, I took comfort in my quiet seething as I walked down to room 121. I beat on the door like a cop with a search warrant. Might as well get this over with as quickly as possible. Courtesy was an on-the-clock skill as far as I was concerned.

"Sir, you missed check-out!"

There was no answer. I knocked louder.

"Sir! We'll charge your credit card for late check-out if you don't come out!"

I couldn't personally do that, but it was close enough to the truth—anything to get the lazy guy off his ass and moving.

But there was still no answer.

I frowned. This was taking up way too much of my time, and other guests had started to open their doors and stare at me. I shrunk away from them and retreated to the front desk. I picked up a universal keycard and marched back to room 121. I knocked one last time.

"Sir, I'm coming in!"

I jammed the keycard into the slot and pushed the door open.

"Sir, I need you to--"

My throat seized around the words. The king-size mattress had been tossed to the other side of the room. It laid flopped against the dresser, threatening to knock the TV from its wall mount. The metal bed frame had been upended against the opposite wall, the headboard leaning on it to support the extra weight.

From the top of the bed frame, a man hung by his neck.

I froze.

As I stood before death, my brain refused to function. I'm not sure how long I stood there, but at one point, my legs started to give out, and I jolted back into focus before I toppled over.

I needed to see if he was still alive. I needed to call someone. Something. I needed to *do* something.

I crossed the threshold, and the skin on the back of my neck tingled like there was a change in air pressure or a draft from the air conditioner.

I approached the hanging man, telling myself he wasn't dead yet. My mind believed that, somewhere deep down. I had to believe that.

The man's neck was wrapped in a bright yellow extension cord. I reached up to try to loosen the cord and touched the man's skin by accident. I snatched my hand back.

He was cold. He really was dead. Dead for a while, based on what the crime shows had taught me.

My stomach sank. This was the closest I had ever been to a dead body outside of a funeral. I didn't want to look, but I couldn't pull my eyes away.

The eyes were bloodshot, filled with red, and staring at nothing. Still wet. Unblinking.

And then he moved.

I jumped back, a strangled yelp leaping from my throat. My heart thrummed in my ears, and my breathing came in painful gasps. It took a long moment of stillness for me to realize that the hanging man hadn't actually moved, but rather a small notebook had slipped out of his hand and hit the floor.

I knelt and picked up the notebook. It wasn't much bigger than my hand, bound in dark faux leather with an elastic band holding it closed. I backed up toward the door, turning the notebook over in my hands, not wanting to be close to the hanging man but also strangely fixated on the object left behind by his corpse. I shouldn't be touching this. I knew that. But that didn't relieve my curiosity.

"Tim! Where are you? Why isn't that guest out of my room yet?"

I jumped at the sound of Josh's voice, shoved the notebook in my pocket, and rushed out of the room.

"What are you doing?" Josh shouted from down the hall, throwing his hands up in the air.

"He's dead," I blurted.

Josh stopped. "What?"

"Dead. Hanged." My words came out choked as if an extension cord was wrapped around my own neck.

I kept walking, looking straight ahead. My face felt tight, and my stomach rolled with nausea. I needed to go.

Josh blinked, seeming to struggle at processing what I had said. "Aw, shit," he mumbled, pushing past me and running to the door of room 121.

"Rita! Somebody! Call 911!" I heard him shout somewhere behind me.

44

I just kept walking until I was out the front door. Nobody stopped me. I climbed into my twenty-year-old Chevrolet, and I pulled out of the motel parking lot. I took the ramp onto I-35 and headed south toward home. The brown, flat, almost desert of east Texas stretched out to either side of my car, dry and barren besides an occasional smattering of farmland plugged into the weak life support of an irrigation system.

And I felt like a bug on a piece of cardstock. On display and exposed for whatever wanted to look. I didn't know what I thought was looking, but that didn't help me shake the feeling. It just made it worse.

The interstate flowed through a tiny town, barely a blip in the landscape. I pulled off at the exit and made my way over the backroads until I came to a gravel driveway patched with dry scrub and pulled in beside the tiny, age-stained trailer I called home.

I staggered out of my car, squinting at the oppressive sunlight, and fumbled with my keys until the front door opened and let me inside. It was nearly noon, but it was past time for nocturnal creatures like me to sleep.

I peeled off my shirt—I was drenched in sweat despite my car's A/C—kicked off my shoes and fell into bed. Without lifting my face from the pillow, I dug my wallet, keys, and phone out of my pockets and dropped them in the loose vicinity of the bedside table.

As I drifted off to sleep, the wide, burning eyes of the hanged man loomed in the front of my mind. They faded in and out with my consciousness. And I swear they blinked.

Fluttering lights swirl around my head. I gaze at them dumbly as I trudge deeper into a forest of murk and mist. The smell of old leaves and rot fills my nostrils. The branches of blue spruce trees reach out to tickle my face with their needle fingers. Behind them, aspens tremble in the silent air, golden leaves dull and somber. The colors mingle in watercolor blotches. The lights are gone. Were they ever there?

I walk deeper.

It's dark. I can see the light through the embrace of shadowing leaves, but it feels like nighttime.

I walk among the roots, the pinecones, and the sweetgum seeds. The thorns and thistles draw back silently to give my feet clear ground. There is no sound: no chittering bugs or singing birds. There is only a sturdy hum like the harmony of mountain roots and the blood of the earth.

The trees begin to thin, but still, no light reaches the rotting leaves and snaking briar vines near my feet. Mountains appear in the sky beyond the trees, slicing black tooth silhouettes against the white sky that gives no light. The slow grinding of stone on stone reaches my ears, and the ground under my feet begins to rumble, as though the bones of the earth are stretching, flexing metamorphic muscles grown cold with age.

I try to continue toward the mountain. Its mass captivates my attention, and I cannot look away. But the ground quakes grow violent. It's hard to keep my footing.

I go on anyway.

The trees lean away now, creeping back from the growling hulk of stone looming above. Even the thistles move past me, retreating from the mountain, huddling low to the earth.
The ground is barren and rocky, and still, there is no light. But I keep walking.

The mountain stretches impossibly high, breathing for the first time in thousands of years. Millions? It pulls me. I want to go there. There is nothing but the mountain. It is all. I need to see it. I need to be there.

The mountain shivers. A great eye opens on its face—miles of white sclera shimmer beneath the rock. Capillaries like rivers flow and twitch under its surface. The eye looks up to the white sky that gives no light, and the sky goes dark. There is only the eye. Oval of white surrounding a circle of black. The pupil quivers, shudders, and shifts down. Toward me.

The notebook slipped from my fingers and smacked into the linoleum, skittering away. I jolted and nearly fell forward off my bed. I must've fallen asleep sitting up. I swore I had fallen into bed, but obviously, I had to have been remembering wrong.

My skin was cold and covered in goosebumps. My head spun with vertigo as I recovered from being awoken from a dream that felt real.

The notebook leaned against the far wall, with its black shell and creamy underbelly. A shiver ran up my spine, the kind that forces its way through your body when you're being watched. I knew I was alone. I was safe. Why did I feel this way?

I stood and snatched up the notebook, rubbing sleep from my eyes with my other hand. It was dark in my room, only a faint gray outline showing around the edges of the curtains. I lifted the notebook and turned it over. Its textures were rough and prominent under my fingers, and the paper scratched at my skin.

I couldn't see the writing on the notebook's pages, but I knew what was there. I knew what the hanged man had written. The eyes were there. The mountain was there. He had seen something. He had known something. And something had seen him. It was a secret, and I knew the whisper.

Something vibrated, pulsing below the floor, and stimulating the soles of my cold, bare feet. My brain itched.

I tugged a burnt orange hoodie over my head and rushed out the door. Watercolor blotches of green and blue and gold swirled in the back of my mind.

I drove my old Chevrolet through the twilight, past the big city, and westward toward the mountains. It was far, but I didn't notice. I turned onto roads seemingly randomly, but something was pulling, buzzing in my head. *It* wanted me in those mountains. The secret was there. It was there for me. I wanted to be alone, but it had other ideas.

Hours later, as my beat-up sedan wound its way up the narrow, treacherous roads, and the night reached in, barely restrained by my dingy headlights, I looked, and I saw it.

I pulled over on a road with no shoulder. I left the engine running, forgotten. Gravel shifted under my bare feet. Hadn't I been wearing shoes? I didn't feel the sharp rocks as I walked out to the sudden drop at the edge of the road, marked with an obligatory and disappointing guardrail.

The forest was dark and silent. The mountain was black. The moonlight would not touch it.

This was not a dream. This was more.

Something in my head itched. My eyes began to vibrate. The scene grew blurry, and I moved forward, squinting to see better.

The edges of the mountain shook. I climbed over the guardrail to get closer. I heard the bones of the earth grinding and scraping, arthritic joints groaning under tectonic plates.

Behind me, my car alarm went off. That shouldn't have happened, I thought. I leaned closer, trying to see the black mountain. I wanted to see what it had for me, what was waiting there for me.

My foot plunged through space. I fell.

It was darkness.

I awake in the night. Pine needles scratch my neck. A stone bruises my lower back. I sit up, my muscles aching. Everything is black. I am surrounded by the scent of old leaves, earth, and rot. I look around, searching for light, for something, but there is only darkness. I look up. There is a hole, like the opening of a cave, jagged and rocky. The sky is there. It's white, but it gives no light.

Something leans over the opening—a silhouette of eyes.

Watching.

Knowing.

Seeing.

My mind wants to recoil from this thing, but I can't. I have to see it.

The dark thing lurches over the ledge, clinging to the rock like an insect. It pitches forward and crawls down into the dark, and I see it only by the liquid white sclerae of its eyes.

The stone rumbles as the eyes descend. Rocks clatter to the ground around me. The echoes sound like screams. The pupils grow larger and larger as the eyes come closer.

More eyes join the first pair. The silhouette of them crawls over the earth. Silent. They do not blink, and they all fix on me. I feel them watching me, seeing me.

I see now. I see the secret waiting for me. It's the truth that our parents wanted us to know. The sermon our pastors preached to us every Sunday. It's the same, but more. It's not Santa, or the Tooth Fairy, or Jesus, or the devil. It's more than that. They were right. They just didn't know how. There is *always* someone watching.

The nerves in my skin electrify. My brain itches with fire. My head buzzes. The eyes loom over me now, and I can feel them vibrating, churning.

They pull me in.

I worked the late shift because it suited me to be alone. Alone. Sitting at the front desk, "keeping watch" during the night, only interacting with the occasional wide-eyed patron. True, the view of a white, lightless parking lot through a set of glass doors left a lot to be desired, but I was the only living thing in the building. No micromanagement, no coercion to look like I'm constantly working. I was free to watch. To sketch and sketch the watching eyes on motel notepads all night long.

Except now, the eyes are there, not just in my notepads. They watch. They know. They can come anytime they want. Now, I'm not alone.

I'm never alone.

AUTHOR BIO

Cory Mason is an author of all fiction genres, but he has a soft spot for the weird and psychological variety of horror. His life's goal is to leave behind a cardboard box of ragged notebooks filled with disturbing scribblings, to be rediscovered in some estate sale or thrift store donation bin. He also writes film and comic reviews for scifiandscary.com. When not writing, Cory can be found working on various film productions. He currently belongs to a long-haired tabby cat named Timb.

SHE WHO BINDS THE BONES

M.S. SWIFT

I am rising and falling to endless music; the boat's tapping, creaking, and groaning accompanies the splash of water against the hull. I inhale the musk of the sea and watch the wind strum the skin of each wave until I am inseparable from the ceaseless swell of the ocean.

Out here, I can see the whole of our island. In less than two years, when I come of age, it will all be mine: the clifftop castle, the gardens laid out on the south-facing slopes with their orchard fringe, the fields plowed onto the lower ground, the meadows and patches of woodland that run down to the marsh that separates us from the mainland beyond.

Four of us run this estate together: Me, Old Sarik, who consults the celestial spheres and who instructs me on all matters he considers necessary for a future ruler; Marna, whom I help in the kitchen and in the upkeep of the chambers that we use; and Tileson, who fishes, catches rabbits in the meadows, and twice a year takes us in his rowing boat to the market in the village up the coast.

Sometimes I find myself watching the bubbling pot whilst Marna sings or, when the sun has risen over the Northern tower, I descend into the gardens to lie in long grasses that are as soft as sand. As the petals of the flowers span the sun's light, I find my gaze drawn to the shadowed rent in an old tree or to the darkness under an overhanging log, and I coil into a soft, welcoming stillness across which the bright day passes until it seems that the sun-girt earth peers through my eyes. At such times I hear or dream a faint song slipping across the gardens. It is of such scintillating sweetness that it might be breathed from the burnished land. Should I stir to seek the source of such music, it fades into the sounds of the woods or the far sea, but if I surrender to it, time falls still, and the world becomes a play of light and color hanging within darkness.

On one occasion, when I had descended to soothe the monthly pain and had passed into that delicious stillness, I traced the song until I found a satyr-like figure carved into a rock among the undergrowth. Its giant legs burrowed like roots into the soil, and I imagined them writhing sinuously down into the very depths of the earth. The flowing arms were clustered with fanning leaves and feathers, and its paws held pipes close to its parted lips. Since then, I have found more figures hidden in the gardens, the orchards, and even the meadows beyond— all carved from outcrops of rock. Old Sarik, one of the few taught to read when my Great Grandfather ruled, named them "Giants Lucky." It was he who instructed me after Mother died; he showed me the books that crumbled in the library. But often, his eyes would peer into years long past, and he would talk of greater days.

He told me that the Giants Lucky brought fertility to the estate and that we should let them dream security into our lives. His words made sense to me, for I knew that when I slept or drowsed, those images lived and that it was they who gave voice to the blissful flowering after winter's grind, of light born from darkness, and of the softness of night that summons the stars from beyond the veils of the sun.

There have been other times when I stand upon the easternmost corner of our battlements and watch as each rebuffed wave twists, prowls, and slips hissing back into the deep once more. The mood will often take me to unmoor Tileson's boat from where it bucks on the jetty and guide the oars through the swell. Once clear of our bay, I mate the sail with the breeze until our island blends with the mainland coast, and I lower the sail again to drift, rising and falling, the slow expanse and contract of the waves belying the fury with which they splinter against the rocks in which our great walls are rooted.

Our home is that of the Dranul line in the far North, away from the Imperial Palace on the Sunset Seas or the wealthy trading ports of the mild south. It was a far grander house when I was a child, with many servants waiting on my parents and their frequent guests.

It is over nine years since my parents were laid in the family vault. Our once plentiful herds and flocks are lost to pox, the estate's income has collapsed, the numbers of servants have dwindled, and the guests are no more. The families once allied to ours spend much of the year in their southern residences. We are content to be forgotten here.

It is long since our sails glowed atop the waves and sailed to the outer isles and lands of the North in search of furs and precious stones mined in the mountains of ice. The last of our great vessels was beached three years ago, and Tileson has long since stripped it of its metal and wood. My mother was the only daughter of her parents and was, by Sarick's account, a disappointment for that reason until her mind and personality developed. It was she who taught me to handle a boat when I was hardly out of infancy.

As we sailed along our coast, she would tell me of her kin who were rooted in the isles and coasts of the North. They who were dark of complexion and eye, befitting their allegiance to the sea and the gloomy sky. It was they and the night who built the ancient rings that are said to stand on the edge of the world, and it was they who had claimed the symbol of the dragon as their own.

When she spoke thus, I felt the strength of our battlements as they defied the fury of both the assailing waves and the raiders that rode those tides. Spring after spring, the attackers were met by our fierce-eyed men until eventually their plundering force was spent, and the invaders settled gratefully into the Northern isles granted them by the Dranul. Once blood was bonded in wedlock, the emperor himself gave my mother's ancestors this land for perpetuity in recognition of their watch over the Northern seas.

Once she came of age, my mother agreed to a match in the hand of Igga Losna of the Northern Isles. His fair hair and blue eyes spoke of his ancestry; his people loved the sun that melted the ice and warmed the sail-swelling winds in the spring skies. Our banner, with its image of the sun and moon hung in balance and of an ocean's serpent, was created at that marriage.

My father told me when one star slips through the clouds at night, it is beacon enough to guide the sailor. He told me that I was his star, for I was the only child born a Dranulosna. If they had ever felt cheated of a dynasty, my parents did not reveal it to me and any bitterness they may have felt they have taken to the vault.

The tomb was established four generations ago and stands within sight of the sea; carefully carved fissures in its roof admit the sea breeze. There is an altar to the gods there, and each day Old Sarick leads us in prayers to the mighty ones, and to their mother, the Great Goddess who Binds the Bones, and to the shades who wait for me in Her gloomy realm. When his voice moans through the tomb, the wind whines through the darkness in reply.

"A sail, a sail!"

Marna's voice called from a window in the keep. I was in the fields gathering meadowsweet and bay for the thresh flooring. When she called again, I dropped my sickle and ran for the walls.

I hardly remembered any sail gliding into the bay beneath our

54

fortress. Marna loved to recall the days when the emperor himself arrived in a fleet with sails of gold. I was a baby when the castle came alive with his court and their daily tournaments, feasting and dancing through the night. Her eyes would stare into the past as she saw our halls bright with torchlight, gold thread gleaming in the light, the faces of men and women shining in merriment.

My heart fluttered like the serpent banner when I beheld the vessel approaching under the morning sun. It was a fine and well-kept ship. In those moments, when I watched the men working the sails or manning the oars below deck, my life was in the hands of the ocean whose waves ferried our blessed vessel into our harbor.

They lowered a rowing boat once the anchor was weighed, and I hurried down to the quayside. Marna joined me equally delighted, but Tileson and Old Sarick stood eyeing the approaching vessel with caution.

It was young men in fine clothes who approached us, swords hanging at their sides. Their smiles were broad, and their eyes reflected the glare from the water. The first bore a scroll bound with the Imperial print and pronounced glad tidings for the house of Dranulosna. Old Sarick took the parchment. He confirmed that the water would take their boat, and to my wonder, the vessel with its brightly painted woodwork and the image of the Sol Invictus on its prow slid into port at my harbor.

The first of the men introduced himself as Wynius Lundcern of the house of that name. He bowed low and stated that both he and his bondmen were pledged to serve me. In his wake, a maidservant trailed who hung her head submissively when Wynius stated that she would tend to him at the table.

Whilst myself and Marna prepared rooms above the great hall, and Tileson hunted rabbits for our feast, Old Sarick and Lundcern retreated to the tower where the seal on the scroll was broken. When eventually they emerged, Old Sarick was grim and weary, but Lundcern appeared in great spirits and composed himself with great charm.

"The Lundcerns are indeed an old family with much land. Wynius is a younger son of that line. However, his exploits in service of the High Priest of Deva have won him a great boon. His Imperial Majesty has granted him this castle and its lands together with your hand in marriage."

Old Sarick spoke to me in the kitchen whilst the men drank their ale in the hall, their voices echoing. I could not comprehend what he was telling me, I had often dreamed of a gallant man who sailed into our harbor, but I had never contemplated a marriage sprung upon me in such a fashion. The laughter and deep voices thumped above us. I had never conceived that the castle would be taken from us and given to another.

"His Majesty has revoked the ancient statute that granted land to the Dranuls. He needs a greater tax yield and more fortresses along the coast," Sarick added.

I did not know what to say. Marna inquired about the legal basis of such a decree.

"I shall study the laws to ascertain whether the perpetuity of the original grant can be over-ruled. On this will rest the basis of an appeal. For now, we must accept our guests as they are many and well-armed...."

Old Sarick had never drawn a sword, and though all of us had swung sickle or scythe at harvest, we could never face such a body of men. Tileson was sent to the High Priest at Deva to confirm the charter. He returned two moons later with word that it was indeed the will of the emperor that my hand be pledged to that of Wynius Lundcern. For the first time since the year of my parent's passing, I felt a profound sense that I was alone in the world.

"In the absence of your father, his majesty claims he shall grant you your future welfare," Sarick stated. The tears that eased forth at these words were painful; all I had ever known, all that I was, had been signed away from me.

During the months after his arrival, Wynius spoke courteously.

Still, haughtiness had crept into the manner of his men whilst the fair-haired servant who attended my future husband regarded me with the eyes of a gannet when Marna tossed fish guts into the sea. They surveyed the buildings and grounds, with their clerk keeping notes on a scroll. Old Sarick accompanied them, answering their questions about the land.

Several days later, the household was assembled in the hall. I was directed to a chair on the dais behind Wynius as he outlined his plans for the land. He granted that I could keep my gardens for private use; however, the remainder of the grounds were to be harnessed to produce food for a future garrison.

The forge was heated again as the armory was to be restocked, and plans were drawn for a shipyard on the southern shore beneath the orchards. Although the chambermaid was responsible for recruiting more household servants, we all had to work harder on the land, and I had scant time to spend on the sea or reclining under the gaze of a Giant Lucky in my garden. Wynius preferred to have the greenery shorn back, and it took much persuasion to preserve my gardens in their semi-wild state.

After the strangers arrived, Sarick took me down into the crypt for only the third time in my life. There were carvings of my parents on the wall above their tombs. My father's likeness was as I pictured him and my mother as I never had. He stood amid a gilt orb, his hair streaming in its rays. His eyes were sky blue as he swung a scythe against sheaves of wheat, casting minute golden orbs towards the ground; the lower grains became pale, creased globes, rather like skulls falling amongst each other into heaps at his feet.

My mother stood on a clifftop, the moon behind her illuminating waves. Her expression was impassive; however, her eyes glinted, reflecting a golden disc adorned with a spiraling pattern. One finger of the hand which held the disc was raised toward the stars, and another pointed down toward the ground, where a serpent coiled around her leg.

"Look at them both, your forebears. See your mother: the source of your physical existence, your nurturer, she who issued you to the yoke of life; it is she who can guide you through this life and perhaps beyond, the gods willing," Old Sarick whispered.

We spent some time at their tombs, the breeze playing through the gloom, before we moved to where my grandparents rested beneath similar carvings-he as Mars and she as Venus. Old Sarick explained the carvings were force and love, balancing one another; expansion and contraction; and the endless death and renewal of all.

The summer of that year passed into a damp autumn and a bitter winter. The winds raged from the North, and their bitterness settled within the castle. I was another year toward my adulthood, and over our meals, Wynius began to talk of marriage in the same tone that he discussed the yields of wheat or apples. The wind moaned in the chimneys when he spoke, and his maid poured wine with eyes of ice.

The following spring, blossom had been cast on the wind and the morning sun rested in the fresh leaves before I next found time to walk in the orchards. My heart was glad for the first time in months until I heard the voice of my lord.

I hung back, listening through the foliage. My lord's voice paused, and there was laughter. Through the shifting leaves, I could see him lying with his chambermaid in the grass. I was shocked at their brazenness and wondered if such behavior had been common. As I looked, her eyes latched onto mine, and she regarded me with the self-satisfied indolence of a cat basking in the summer sun.

I stole away through the briars and secreted myself in the shade of a willow tree. There I prayed to the Great Mother who lends the green leaves their beauty and who is the power behind sun and sea. Tears of rage burst through my silent words until, eventually, I slipped into a reverie.

As I slept, I writhed sensuously among soft, sweet-scented petals. A

58

tall figure approached as smoothly as a wave passing through the land. It knelt close beside me and leaned in, its curving horns parting the hanging flowers as it regarded me.

After a while, it began to pipe: a thin, high sound that set the petals shivering and lifted the delicate stems of the beech leaves above us. The tempo increased, flurries of notes billowing forth until the leaves strained and raced across the wind. As if in response, a serpent emerged from a hollow log lying near the willow roots and passed writhing by my feet. I followed its path through green archways, around ridged roots, and into bright grass and felt myself flowing inevitably toward bare flesh.

I snapped awake.

The chambermaid's screams rang from the tree trunks. I sat up tense. My lord's voice was now shouting in anger. I shifted to my feet and stole through the undergrowth as her cries died away. I could see my lord through the leaves. I crept closer and leaned around a trunk.

The girl was glassy-eyed and lay shivering. Her side was punctured and bled fat orbs that glistened in the grass. Wynius looked upon her in concern. His fist was fixed around the neck of a serpent whose tail twisted and thrashed. The girl shuddered, and her eyes came to rest upon mine, and she hissed and spat, "witchery, witchery...."

Wynius turned to me, his eyes desperate. The serpent hissed once, and then its head was wrenched off. Droplets of blood flicked from the stump as the body dropped and lashed against the ground, knotting itself in endless movement until spent, it sank beneath the grass. Wynius kneeled against the girl and then turned toward me.

"Dead. Dead. Was that you piping? Charming the snake? No? Where are your pipes?" His voice rose from a whisper as he spoke.

He flung the serpent's head through the undergrowth and held her wrist awhile. The breeze lifted the leaves and scattered the scent of the sea around the orchard. In time, he let the hand fall and turned in silent fury toward me.

"You charmed the snake from its lair, and she called you a witch. I name you an enemy of the God who slays serpents," he hissed.

"I play no pipes," I replied.

He stared into my eyes and then kicked away from me, "then where is your piper?"

He wheeled away, dragging me behind him as he hurtled through the trees in the direction of where I had slept. He kicked out at ferns, still unwinding from their tight buds. The shivering of the leaves suggested the passage of a person, and he hurried off until he came to a stone Giant half-hidden among silver birch trees. He attempted to fling it to one side. Finding it carved from an outcrop of rock, he kicked at it, crumbling the face, and turned snarling,

"What is this thing? This deformed, monstrous image?"

"Don't you touch that. It is ours, part of our land, the Dranuls," I snapped back.

He paused, taken aback by my anger, and then he leaned his face into mine and quietly said, "this land is mine, and I am a man of *the* God. This statue is an abomination before His radiance, and I will destroy it."

With that, he turned away and stalked through the silent gardens. I waited till his retreating figure had gone. Then I pulled the greenery down over the image and prayed to the Great Goddess that She protect our Giants Lucky. I spent the rest of the day at the Giant, and no men came to raise their steel against it.

That evening I confided in Old Sarick in the kitchen. He spoke with a heavy heart, "there is an island, some two days sail from here. It was the ancient burial isle of your mother's ancestors. It is a place where old enchantments may still veil its cliffs from unwelcome eyes. Should it become necessary, take Tileson's boat. It has fresh water and all else you may require stowed within. Set your course northeast of where the sun rises in early summer, and by evening, turn away from the path of the hunter

60

through the skies."

I dreamt of my mother for the first time in years; I yearned with the plaintive power of the gull's cry to be borne to the shadowed strand where she stood waiting for me.

Marna woke me the next morning with ill tidings: Wynius had smashed into our vault overnight. He had defiled the engravings of my parents and swept their bones into a sack which he flung down the old well on the cliff's head. In their place, he laid the body of his maid. Marna did not need to tell me that his men were to move against the gardens that day. I took a hurried leave of my friends and made for the quayside.

My craft was already beyond arrow shot when my flight was discovered. I could see a huddle of people gathering on the quay and made out Old Sarick's thin, robed form in their midst. He was at the edge where the waves plunder and prowl against the rocks. Faces were turned toward me, but I could hear no cries above the sough of the wind and the slump of the waves.

A blade was brandished in the sunlight, and a rowing boat started after me, but I was gathered by the wind and ferried across the swell. Gulls circled in undulating loops, their svelte forms flashing in the sun, the waves vanished in the reflected light before breaking away again, and the waning moon hung in the sky as I played the sail against the wind.

I thought of my parents' dear bones as I sailed beyond the battlements of my castle. Torn from their rest, they were now in the dark heart of the cliff, under the water that nurtured the roots of the trees that grew around the castle.

Sarick paid for my escape with his head. His lean figure flailed like a puppet on the quayside. Wynius, recognizable in his robes, gestured at me with his sword raised. Moments passed before the blade abruptly cleaved in the far distance. I was too intent upon my escape to register the horror of that act, and before long, all was ocean.

I had never been so far out to sea that all land vanished and only fields of shifting waves remained. A westerly wind flurried through the sails, and the water was alive with serpents of light undulating beneath the morning sun.

When night came and stars tracked across the sky, I looked for the horn and bow of the hunter, as his great shape formed from a mesh of stars. I adjusted course and sailed through the night.

Swelling dawn silhouetted a serpentine ridge of land on the horizon ahead. I prayed to the imprint of the moon to guide me to a sandy cove. Birds shrieked from their roosts on sheer cliffs as I approached. With no sign of access to the isle, I circled the cliffs and soon spotted a cave at sea level.

As I neared, I found it an artificial opening flanked by mighty forms sculpted from the rock. Looking up into the faces glowering through wisps of cloud, I was reminded of the Giants of home, and I was reassured enough to guide my vessel close, lowering the sail when a current caught me and drew me into darkness.

I drifted between walls of rock toward a distant light that grew into an open-air harbor. An outcrop of rock formed a natural quayside, and a host of giant figures carved into the wall behind reassured me that I had arrived at the place of my ancestors. I moored my craft as best I could and disembarked.

The voice of the sea was insistent against the cavern walls; its waves leapt over the weed-smothered stone, urging me up the steps cut into the walls. The wind moaned gently in the tunnel behind. I ascended into sunlit grass blowing on the clifftop and the noise of many unseen birds on the cliff-face below. To my left, an arrangement of rough, hulking stones stood overlooking the sea, whilst to my right crude stone buildings were gathered in a close circle before a green mound.

The atmosphere was bleak, yet I was reminded of my mother's

62

portrait in the crypt, and I felt her presence around me in a way that I had not done for years. I moved to the clifftop and stood as she had upon that headland. Sunlight fell around the shadow I cast across the sea, and as I stood there, I blessed the serpent which rose from its rest to strike at that woman.

The stones upon the headland were arranged in a wide, circular pattern with three larger, central monoliths leaning into each other conspiratorially. Whilst I walked among them, I had the impression that I walked among crude depictions of our giants. Some were twisted and hunched close to the ground, others loomed above me, and all bore bulbous swellings and rutted crevices that creased into large faces. The buildings nearby were round huts that though long abandoned, would still afford shelter from the elements.

Aligned with that settlement, a stone door frame set into the mound was visible. When I crouched before that portal, I felt a little afraid for the first time since I had arrived. The island did not feel inhabited. The birds on the cliffs were plentiful and did not mind me, and there was no sign of recent habitation. Yet as I faced that low corridor dug into the earth, I felt a sense of expectancy. A faint whistling and moaning was audible from within. I imagined people gathered in the darkness until I noticed it answered the ebb and flow of the breeze. Eventually, I stole enough courage to venture in.

Three chambers opened from that passage, and I found to my unease that each hosted a multitude of carefully arranged skulls. Save for several horned cattle, the skulls were human. As numerous as barley grains, they were carefully arranged in rows on stone piles and in niches carefully sited in the stone walls. Some, adorned with precious stones, painted marks, or even animal horns and tusks, were afforded prominent positions. Some collapsed into dust, and others had lost their jawbones or lay upended on the floor. However, most stared blankly at me through clenched teeth. The wind moaned through the darkness, and each hollow dome and each empty socket piped faintly in reply. I returned their gaze until something of that blankness and stillness slithered into me.

When I left, I was convinced that that place was no house of the dead, and as birds wheeled across the sky, I thought of my parents' remains and wondered if they too sang beneath the waters of the well. I ate the provisions from the boat and spent the remainder of the day exploring the island. Shellfish were available in a small, shallow cove, and I drank from a spring rising on the eastern headland. I gathered fallen wood in the apple thickets that clad the south-facing meads, and with supplies from the boat, I was able to light a fire in the most substantial of the houses.

The light of the setting sun fell across the stones, softening their features and drawing rich red and golden timbres from them. They must have made a magnificent sight to vessels that approached at this time: richly arrayed beings standing in greeting upon the hill. I thought of the moon when she rolls across the horizon and how her light must gleam like bone among those stones.

The constant sound of wind and waves made me feel at home on that little isle. Their voice kept at bay the horror from which I had fled, and I curled to sleep by the fire.

In time, the whine of the wind shifted into deliberate harmonies that became the piping of one among the stones on the headland. A light like a small candle woke within me, and I found myself in the company of a familiar being, a stem-slender and earth-rooted being whose flowing limbs were clad in curling pelt and whose head was crowned with summer-leaves that shivered with his sweet piping. It was the song of summers gone, of the beauty of the moonrise over sea and stone. It was a song that called to me from across the sea, summoning me from my shelter out into the heavenly splendor swelling beyond.

I emerged, and with the wind booming through the tombs and the dead whining in return, the piping melted from my dreams into reality. I

64

could no longer see the piper, but I knew that I was in the presence of one whose enchanting music welled from the earth in the castle gardens. The voice was no longer audible, yet I felt that it spoke in the breeze billowing around me and the sea plundering the rocks at the foot of the cliffs. When I walked toward the stones on the headland, I walked toward the one who called me.

The moon had indeed risen, and in the soft light, grooves and patterns carved into the stones became visible. My eye traced a particular spiraling pattern to its center and back out again. As I did so, earth and sky broke into patterns of light that pulsed to the hollow piping. The contours of the stones became as clusters of fire burning over a skull-hollow blankness, and I found myself shivering until a feeling of peace and stillness expanded within me.

There came a time when I attuned to the sonorous boom of the wind through the mound and the faint whistling of the skulls within. It was the dead of the earth replying from their hollow home to the voice of the sky—the sounds distorted before clarifying into crying voices, pulsing drums, and the wailing of many pipes.

The air grew heavy, and the shadows of writhing figures flowed among the burning stones. Nothing was static: shadow and light shifted around me, and I was entwined among dancing shadows until giants like those of our gardens woke into pulsing life and sonorous cries and unfurled their long limbs from the night. Gnarled faces with bulbous features flickered through the rout, faster and faster we went until my skin broke hot against the blank surface of the stones. I felt no pain. My body rolled and crashed like the waves beneath the cliff, and darkness fell across me: a blank, earth black, hollow tree darkness that held me tightly and settled a luxurious stillness over me.

A lessening of the gloom arose in time, and fragments of soft light were revealed until they coalesced into a glow like the sun through a sea fog.

The light strengthened until beyond its radiance, a vast figure became apparent. If the depths of night, sea, and earth were to concentrate their immensity into a union, then such a being may walk forth.

Illuminated by her inner light, I beheld the Great Goddess. In the radius of Her being, I was unmoored. She was the wave that lifted me into the light. She was the sea from which I rose. She was the sun before whom I circled.

I was the void, and She was the fire of the stars burning within.

When She began to sing, the darkness echoed. Though I heard no words, layers of sweet sound built until it seemed the void piped to Her, and from that music, sea and shore and sky came into being. Her presence remained visible to me behind the world, and before Her, a shape emerged from the sea waves. It formed into a head I recognized as that of Wynius Lundcern. His eyes were rolled up into his skull, and his mouth hung open. I saw too the heads of his companions, all severed and bound to his as if on a chain. A fury burst within me along with an urge to gather this chain and dance across it, to press myself against it like a serpent glorying in its victory. Through the fog of rage, the countenance of the Great Goddess reappeared to look in love upon me.

Awareness returned with the rising sun. I paid no heed to the shreds of greenery plastered to my scabbing cuts or the knots tangled in my hair, for a familiar voice sounded over the dawn waters. It was the cry of my mother calling me home, and I felt within me the great stillness of mind of one who has passed beyond mortality into the presence of the Great Goddess.

Once the boat was rowed from the tunnel, a friendly wind caught the sails and bore me to the open sea. The same wind worried at my wounds and sewed flecks of blood through the heaving waters for a while. With the breeze behind me, I made swift progress, and by the time the sun glowering in the west framed the land, I saw once more the towers and banners of my castle.

"I have come to claim my birth rite and my marriage," I called to the guards who had gathered on the quayside. Through lantern light, they stared in astonishment at the apparition which drifted closer to them. Some laughed, but those who saw the hollow darkness that lay behind my eyes lowered their spears toward me. A horn sounded from the battlements where the serpent banner no longer flew. The lord of the castle approached at speed, and his retainers drew behind him.

"You were lost at sea. No marriage can proceed," the lord called through a nest of spears.

"My marriage is not to you," I replied as the waves buoyed me against the quayside. The darkness that had lain bound within the ancestral bones now lay within me. It cradled me, and through its comforting stillness, I felt rather than heard shrill whistling from under the earth.

I raised my arms into the wind, and everything shivered. The world flickered once, and the presence of the Goddess rose around me like a black wave. I embraced my return to Her.

Though my body seemed suddenly frail, She spoke through me and the darkness answered with a multitude of voices that whistled, shrieked, and groaned.

The quayside and castle strained and broke into streaks of light that sparked across a gaping gulf. The shapes of men, the great castle, and even the sea and sky were like flickering images mapping dense darkness.

The blades that were thrust toward me vanished. The lord's voice barked and failed as the world, unmoored, broke into a brief burning across the void.

The All-Mother had thrown wide the gaping mouth of eternal night, and the land of shadow fell across the land of men. The restless ocean, the sheer rocks, the vaulting ramparts, and even the stars above were all cradled in a dark as expectant as turned earth and as comforting as the hollow mound. I watched myself step into this flattened world from those depths, moving through the scattered guards on the quayside toward the stairway into the castle. I reached the gate into the bailey in time to see his retainers breaking in terror as moaning shadows impressed themselves upon the splintered world.

Marna noticed me amid the confusion and ran to my side, her terrified expression changing to one of wonder and relief. Failing to rally his men, Wynius turned and made for the two of us. He screamed his curses and called upon his god of light as I guided Marna through the far gates into the watching gardens.

All was as a reflection flickering around me, and I sensed a stirring of the shadow deep within. There was an expansive, uncoiling sensation, and from the pregnant blackness of the well on the headland above us, the sodden, headless forms of Old Sarick and Tileson heaved themselves forth and flopped onto the grass.

Ecstasy tightened my limbs, and as Wynius passed through the gate, I felt old bones surface from the shaft and spill onto the earth. Wynius did not see the dead I drew from the whistling darkness until their freezing limbs clamped around him. He screamed helplessly into their hollows. The last of his men leaping for the departing ship or fleeing toward the marsh did not see him borne onto the ramparts where my mother's skeletal hands wielded the blade that sent his head into the hissing waves.

The body of Wynius Lundcern and that of his mistress followed his head onto the sea-shredding rocks. Before our dead took their rest that night, they ensured that the last of his henchmen had fled our isle. Doubtless, they spread tales of the island ruled by a witch queen who conjures spirits bound to the ancestral bones. If their words keep others at bay, then I am satisfied.

Marna and I dwell here still, but we are not alone. The presence of the Great Mother charges the land. From Her depths, the voices of beings half-glimpsed in the crashing tides, the spreading boughs, and the undulating earth sing as faintly and sweetly as the first flowering after frost

or as the light flickering on the endless waves of the dark ocean.

AUTHOR BIO

M. S. Swift writes dark fantasy, contemporary horror, and Victorian 'Straw Punk.' Inspired by the British landscape and folklore, and occult traditions drawn from across the globe, he has been published in more than twenty print and online anthologies by a range of publishers. He has also edited an anthology of teen ghost stories that featured an introduction and contribution from horror icon Ramsey Campbell.

VICTIM

BY NAOMI BRETT ROURKE

I have been lying on the bed for hours, watching as the sun peaked over the top of the curtains, making its slow way down the window glass, first butter yellow, then rose, then red-orange like a flame at noon. Like every other day, today, I am locked in this bedroom.

I am his prisoner. His victim. I move to the floor and lie on my back, staring at the ceiling and watching the dust motes make lazy circles in the light beam. I have nothing to occupy my time but to sit and to wait.

I gulp huge bites when he brings my meals because I never know when my plate will be swept away. I rush my toilet without knowing when I will be thrown out of the bathroom. He kicks me when I displease him and laughs at me when I cry. When I show spirit by running or fighting back, he catches me, cuffs me, or throws me against the wall. He is so much bigger than I am, and I am afraid.

I've tried to learn his language, but it's so guttural and sharp. When I first attempted, he jeered at me so cruelly that I shrank away, turning my back and crying. Then he left. Several days later, after leaving me without food, bathroom, or water, he returned. I had to perform my waste in the

71

corner, and I hid it, ashamed, by covering it with papers and pieces of clothing he had left in the room.

When he finally let me out, I ran for the water and gulped it down. Guzzled it in, barely stopping for breath. The food he gave me was old and crusty, with spots of mold. I didn't care and wolfed it down, but I could barely chew it, and he laughed at my disgust.

When he found my waste, he yelled and booted me. He locked me in my room again, and I threw myself against the door, screaming, crying to get out. I vomited my vile dinner on the floor, and when he finally unlocked the door, I was beaten for that too.

I sit and watch the birds in the trees outside. They flit back and forth, calling companionably to each other. They huddle together to keep warm in the winter, and tiny new chicks are hatched in the spring. I watch them chirp for worms and bat their small wings. The mother bird urges them to fly, and, with my heart in my mouth, I watch as they take their first flight.

I would love to fly with them, to spread my wings and soar up to the blue sky, playing tag with the fluffy clouds, and hide-and-go-seek with the raindrops. Instead, I sit in my room and watch, hungry for their freedom.

Every once in a while, a person will go by, a silver-haired woman limping in a cherry red coat, a young man strolling to his own internal music, a mother and daughter in matching raincoats and rubber boots. I beg them, imploring them, beating on the window, but they don't see me. They don't understand what I'm saying. They speak the same language as the man. They turn their heads, look at me, and ignore me. I don't matter to them. Do I matter to anyone?

The man walks in for his daily bath. I sprint over to the far wall to stay out of his way, and he laughs one sharp, jeering note. He turns the water on full force, and as it cascades into the tub, he disrobes.

I hate looking at him. Grub-like and palely white, with sparse hair up and down his body, he is out of shape with a huge belly and flabby arms, but he is so tall and so massive that he can hurt me regardless. I turn my back, so I don't have to see him.

The water gurgles in the tub, and I think about my thirst. I have had no food or drink since I vomited, and I am weak and pitiful, arms barely strong enough to reach up for help, if there ever was any. I creep over to the door and stand, leaning against the doorframe, watching him lie back in the water.

Strands of black and gray hair trail over his bald spot. His ears are pinned back like an angry cat. His mouth is as flabby as the rest of him and is permanently leering or guffawing or shouting. Tiny piggy eyes of brown are nearly hidden by overgrown black and gray eyebrows, and deep lines cobweb around his eyes, matching the ravine etched on each side of his cruel mouth. He had mammoth shoulders and a colossal-sized back, which the giant tub now hides.

How can I ever hope to escape?

He feels my presence and looks back, calling me, quietly, gently. I do not want to go, but will he refuse me food and water again if I don't? Beat me again? My legs shake, and I can't figure out whether to go to him or stay by the door. Either choice could doom me.

Padding over, I sit just out of arms reach, watching him warily. He soothes me with his words; he entices me with his tone. I don't believe him, though I'm so hungry and thirsty. The thought of a full belly and clear, fresh water lures me.

Though I don't want to, I take a step or two within his reach, and he cups his hand against my cheek and gazes at me. I look miserably into his eyes, tears forming. I don't want to cry in front of him, but I have no choice. I take the last tiny steps and perch myself on the side of the tub. I eye the water. Suddenly, I am seized with the desire to drink his bathwater.

Horrible? Yes. But I'm so thirsty. Without daring to look him in the eyes, I lower my head.

His attention is caught, and he watches me. I dip my face to the water and take a sip. The water tastes strange—rich and salty—but surprisingly, it's not appalling. In fact, it's strangely compelling, and I bend to drink again. I draw it in, and suddenly, I can't get enough. I wallow in the taste. I swallow and swig and slurp.

When I finish, I am confused and back out of the bathroom uneasily. He watches me, his eyes like glass marbles, hard and shiny. I find myself sickened but also drawn to that rich and salty water. He looks at me kindly when he comes out, cleans up the vomit and the waste, and gives me extra time for my dinner.

The next day he comes in for his bath, and I am at the door, waiting. He giggles—one more thing he does to unnerve me—and when the tub is full, I drink. He talks to me, saying words I don't understand, but his tone is gentle and soft.

I'm finally drinking my fill, and I'm content. I am still disgusted with drinking his bathwater, but the taste is beginning to grow on me. I feel my muscles ripple beneath my skin. I feel stronger. I *am* stronger.

Every day, the man invites me in for his bath. Sometimes when he goes out, I creep into the bathtub, lie down, and lick the bottom and the sides of the tub of water. It is despicable, but I do it. I do so love the taste.

Today the man had his bath with me as usual. He reached for something as I was drinking and caught the side of my head, tipping me into the water from the edge of the tub. The tub was wide and big and filled with murky water. I panicked. Liquid filled my mouth, my ears, and rushed down my throat. I took a deep breath and inhaled water into my lungs. I couldn't breathe, and I coughed and gagged.

Grabbing at the nearest thing, I raked him with my nails, trying to get my head above water. Blood welling from his arms, the man bellowed and surged out of the water. He grabbed me by my sodden hair and threw me across the room, and I fell into the corner and huddled there, hacking, gasping. The raspberry-red of his face frightened me, and with a black look, he kicked me as he walked out the door, and it set me to coughing and retching again. I stayed there silently, while great tears ran down my face, nursing my bruised body my thigh from where I hit the corner wall, my stomach where he kicked me.

I stayed in that corner for hours, damp, cold, miserable. After a while, I was thirsty, so I crept over to the tub to see if there was any water left on the bottom, but he hadn't drained the water. It was still there. I pulled myself up on the ledge, bent over, and drank. I pulled my head up suddenly—the water tasted odd. Something I had not tasted before. Rich, richer than the taste from the man's sweat. Salty and tangy with a hint of something else. I bent and took another sip. It sparked my tongue and sent shivers down my spine.

The pleasure was palpable, throbbing. It was a metallic taste, coppery, exotic, spicy. I thought back to when I was in the water, and I fought to get out. I had clawed his arms and torso with my nails until he bled. Blood. It was his lifeblood mixed in with the bathwater, and it was delicious. Just a drop, perhaps. Maybe two. I drank even more than I had before and lay, replete, on my bed.
And then, I dreamt.

Something is happening to me again. I feel different. Powerful. Today the man comes in and runs his bath. I sit very still, watching. He looks at me and disrobes, grunting at me. He steps into the water and leans back, eyes closed. I creep in noiselessly. He opens his eyes and stares at me, and, after a moment of hesitation, he pats the ledge of the tub. I come slowly and gingerly sit, ladylike, waiting. He talks to me, words he knows I do not understand, and smiles. The bathwater is there, and my mouth is already watering for the briny, rich taste of it.

He closes his eyes, and I bend to drink. Suddenly, his hand is on the back of my head, and he thrusts me under the water. I shake my head, but I can't get free. I can't breathe. His other hand is holding my shoulders down, and as much as I struggle, I cannot raise my head above water. My arms flail, and my legs kick, but I cannot get purchase. The tub has turned into an angry ocean, waves crashing over me, punishing me. I feel darkness gnawing at the corners of my mind, and at the last minute of consciousness, I jackknife my legs under me and strike out at him with all my might, at the same time clawing his arms, chest, and face.

Under the water, I hear muffled shrieking, and suddenly I am free. I tumble out of the water, and I sprawl on him as he roars. I stare in shock at the damage my nails have made to his ripped flesh, blood pouring from a dozen wounds, and suddenly I can take no more. I launch myself at his contemptible face, clawing, biting, and screaming. He is shocked and tries to hold my furious wet body, but he cannot. All the abuse, pain, and abandonment come rushing up and give me power beyond my little body. He cannot hold me. I'm too waterlogged and too enraged. I don't care how much he hurts me this time. I don't care if he kills me! But he won't.

He. Won't.

I scream my fury, and his eyes widen, bloodshot and liquid with pain. I see my opening and I take it, slamming my legs against his and crashing my face into the soft tissue beneath his blue-black jaw, in that soft and prickly area where his vein beats blue. Opening my jaws, I bite and bite. Blood cascades down his pallid chest, his flaccid stomach, and into the water. He grabs blindly at me and pulls, trying to break my grip, but I dig my nails into his shoulders and hold on, crescent moons of blood appearing where my fingers find his body.

His arms are getting weaker and weaker, his arms flail and his legs pump weakly, and I clamp my teeth tighter. Blood spurts up from his throat and drenches the wall, drenches me, and it is hot, so hot. When he no longer moves, and the scarlet blood is coursing over his body and mine, when the tub water is crimson with his lifeblood, and he lies pasty and impotent, then, finally, I drink.

I sit outside in the sun and look at the people going past on the sidewalk. They all have somewhere to go. They all have busy lives and don't even glance at me. I am not of them. I never was. Something has grown inside of me, something strong and wild and welcome. It happens every time I have been a victim for too long. I don't know why I am different. I always have been. They either look past me or look at me with pity, or they look at me with something else in mind. These are the best. They look at me and see someone so small. So pitiful. So weak.

But I am not weak.

These people love fragile things. They love to take care of the feeble and the frail. The vulnerable. It makes them feel good, I think, in their not-so-good world—until it goes wrong. Until they feel put upon by the responsibility of caring for someone so needful. Until they long for freedom from their duty. Then they feel powerful. Then they feel obligated to sever their ties with what binds them regardless of the hurt they cause, the bruises they leave, the pain they inflict.

But they are the ones who are weak.

I see a dark-haired man glance at me and then slow his steps and turn. He bends down and talks softly to me. I see the gleam in his eyes, and I know. I look up into his grey eyes and wait. He will take me home and make a prisoner of me. He wants me to be his victim. His kind always does.

Always.

AUTHOR BIO

Naomi Brett Rourke is a writer, teacher, and theatre director. As an author, Naomi has been published in a variety of magazines, journals, and anthologies, including an award-winning story in the best-selling anthology *Straight Outta Tombstone*, and a Christmas story in *The Saturday Evening Post*. Naomi lives near her beloved beach with her husband, Tim. She has three children, three stepchildren, a passel of grandchildren, as well as a dog, two cats, a tortoise, and the myriad of birds that visit every day. Visit her at NaomiBrettRourke.com

Mountain Song

BY MARK TOWSE

The sense of smell.

I can't imagine ever being without it. Here, halfway up the mountain, the air so crisp, a delicious concoction of earth, wood, and wildflowers. Petrichor wafts on the breeze—nature's untainted perfume, potently seductive in the absence of human contamination.

Steady does it.

Yes, perfect shot.

Even in the dull light, the camera lens exaggerates the intricacy of the web, a marvel of engineering decorated by shimmering globes of moisture hanging from the weaving like fairy lights. No sign of the maker. Perhaps it's just hiding, waiting for its prey to ensnare itself in the beautiful deathtrap.

My skin prickles with goosebumps as cool air wraps around it, but I force myself to stay still, taking a moment to enjoy my surroundings. Inhale. I wish Dad were here with me, though. Exhale. I shrug off the backpack, unzip the bottom pocket and take a few glugs of tepid water from the bottle, just managing to fight back the tears. Inhale.

Hard to believe two decades have passed since we were last here.

The mountain carries a special place in my heart; memories of exploring with Dad—the long chats, the laughter, not to mention the awe for his knowledge of its flora and fauna. We called it our "secret mountain"; silly really with the place being visible from town on a clear day, but we rarely spotted others, only the occasional seasoned local.

My father said the mountain had a reputation, a sinister history that spooked most residents into staying away, told me there were reports of an old research facility that used to carry out wacky experiments on God knows what. Although the thought occasionally made my skin crawl, I put it down to a campfire story, urban legend, or just something Dad concocted for kicks. Gossip was never his thing, unlike Mum. Her being such a worrier, we always told her we were going fishing, even threw a couple of old rods in the back of the truck before we left. Sometimes we brought fish home from the market.

God, I miss him.

Mum wouldn't let me come out here on my own, and we had to sell the house shortly after, without Dad's wage coming in. We ended up moving to the other side of the country. I meant to return sooner, but life got busy and hasn't stopped.

Mountain's always been at the back of my mind, though.

I throw the backpack around my shoulders and continue traversing the undergrowth. It's less than thirty minutes since I left the main path, but already it's getting harder to negotiate—thicker, spikier—as if the land is going into self-protection mode.

We were never ones to stay on the path; that was for amateurs, holidaymakers.

Ducking under the occasional spindly arm that seems hungry for skin, I force my way through the ever-thickening scrub. Another web in the tree to my right catches my eye, larger but no less elaborately detailed by the absent architect. My dad could tell me the names of the arachnids just

80

from the shape and structure of their silky lattices. Before he met Mum, he traveled worldwide, writing countless articles for cool magazines. Some of them are on my bookshelf at home, dog-eared, well-loved.

The web's threading is much stronger than I imagined it to be. Even as I apply pressure, it just bows with no signs of snapping. Hard to believe something so small—

No way! There they are! The rocks!

It's as if it was yesterday, the branches framing them just as I remember.

"Race you, Dad!"

I scramble across the uneven ground, jumping over puddles and loose rocks, weaving in and out of overgrown vegetation. An image flashes, so vivid—Dad going flying, his boot getting caught in a skinny offshoot. Christ, he went down so quick and hard, I thought he'd knocked himself out. But then his shoulders began heaving up and down as he got to his feet. Blood dripping from his top lip where his teeth had gone through, the tough bastard was laughing.

Laughing!

It set me off, too, and we didn't, couldn't stop for ages.

They're still there! Oh my God, they're still there.

The scratching on the rock sets me off again, a bout of raw, uncontrollable laughter that makes me feel so incredibly close to him. Tears fill my eyes, a happy sadness that I never want to end. Our initials—such a strong bond forever memorialized.

The connection we had was something I've always wanted to reciprocate with a child of my own. Alas, Jody and I have spoken about starting a family, but she isn't convinced. Her father absconded when she was twelve, shortly after cancer took her mother, and I'm not sure she shares my belief that Dad didn't just leave. If she'd experienced the same level of kinship that I did, she might feel differently. We avoid the conversation for the time being, but it won't go away. Not as far as I'm concerned. It's like a dark cloud, waiting to unleash.

The three rocks were our marker; two giant formations standing side by side, impossibly symmetrical, and another laid across the top as though forming a doorway from one part of the mountain to the other. We used to joke that it was magical, but I could never deny the prickles on the back of my neck and the unique fragrance that transcended even nature's capability when stepping through the doorway. Sounds seemed different on the other side, too, softer, and there was a faint but alluring hum in the air. I know this sounds insane, but I used to think it sounded like the distant song of an angel. It's safe to say that we were both smitten.

We'd sit there on the other side, feasting on the treats Mum prepared for our fishing trip, talking for ages about nothing and everything. After that, we'd begin our journey home. Always with mixed emotions on the way back, part of me relieved to be returning to the car and the predictability of Sunday afternoon, but also an undeniable intrigue, a silly childhood notion that something extraordinary was on the other side of that doorway, further up the mountainside.

I think Dad felt it, too, but he played it down. Anyhow, we made a pact that one day we'd come back when I was older, extending our journey beyond the door. We'd prepare properly, stay the night—tent, matches—the whole nine yards. I made him swear that he'd never come up here without me.

Breathing in its dampness, I run my hands across the rock, noting the web above spanning into a vast sprawling design crossing from one internal corner to the other. Dad would be blown away by this. Hard to make anything out in the blackness, but again, no sign of the artist. Onwards.

Like magic, my senses are once again enhanced as I pass through the doorway—the creak of trees, the flutter of butterfly wings, and the accompanying heady fragrance. Just as I remember, but more.

82

I wonder if Dad felt it this way—so powerful, so seductive. How did he keep this from me? Warmth fills me, my heart rate elevates. I feel freer, lighter, navigating through the undergrowth and thorny shrubs with much more dexterity and—

Damn!

Instinctively, I begin clawing at my waist and legs, following the thread, and tracking it back to the edge of the tree. The web must be four feet high, at least. Thicker than the others, too. Thoughts turn to its owner, and my raking gets more frantic. I imagine it already on me, legs dancing across my skin, fans ready to sink into flesh. Jesus! So much of it; soft, yet impossibly tough. Sticky, too, somehow. What the hell is this thing supposed to be catching?

My body gives out a shudder as I continue to peel it away, eyes darting between the tree's branches. It's probably watching, waiting. Come on!

Imagine the bite on the thing.

Come on! I've just got to—

Free!

I run my fingers through my hair and scratch furiously at the back of my neck, finally doubling over and sucking in air, giggling as I imagine Father standing next to me, mocking my demonstration of bravery.

"Hilarious, Dad."

Composure intact, I lift the camera and take a step back, but the web is still too large to get into focus. A little shuffle, and—Jesus Christ, another one—wrapping around my neck, my ears, my legs even. Frantically, I work at it, kicking out and catching myself a good one on the nose as I blindly swipe at skin that sings with unease. Finally, I thrust forward, working myself free but almost losing balance, only momentum keeping me up. I stagger on, thoughts of the undoubtedly sizable creator scuttling across my body inducing a series of involuntary shudders.

The incline increases, and the sound carrying on the air undoubtedly gets louder and clearer. It's coming from much higher up, although I see nothing but trees and even thicker undergrowth ahead.

Beyond the songbirds and wind rustling the leaves, though, there's an underlying hum that wraps my brain with warmth, an angelic chorus extending my hyperalert state to such an extent it feels as though every hair on my body stands in ovation. The smell that fills my nostrils is intoxicating, stirring something deep within—an excitement and curiosity that goes beyond anything I've experienced before. It's almost as though the mountain is calling me.

Dad. Did you feel this, too? Did you come back without me?

It's haunting, mesmerizing.

Mum said he left, got bored, bailed out, that it was *a dark cloud* that chased him away. Once a traveler and all that. To this day, she still thinks he did a runner, that he couldn't handle suburbia, and that he was likely to be living on the side of a mountain somewhere.

But he wouldn't leave. I know it. We had our bond.

I glance behind, eyeing the doorway of the mountain in the distance. Part of me wants to return to the safety of normality, but like father, like son, I march on. There's magic here. I can feel it. And maybe even answers?

Two more webs stretch out ahead, but I'm getting wise to their likely locations, and I carve a path away from groups of trees and large bushes. Even as the gradient significantly increases and the spindly roots get thicker and more abundant, I'm making good ground. My reward is an even more heightened state of awareness—the music, the fragrance—the magic.

Wait! What was that?

Over there, on that web. Something moved, I'm sure of it!

I afford myself a slower pace, warily trudging towards the two trees. Jeez, this one must be about five feet wide and—maybe seven feet tall? I edge forward, daring not to get too close. I'm sure as hell I saw something;

heard something. Slowly, I make my way around the left trunk, blood pounding in my ears and eyes darting frantically from branch to branch.

Nothing.

I hold my breath and inch forward through the thick forest carpet. A little more.

Something scuttling, close. Heart racing, I snap my head around, and it stops immediately.

Where is it? What is it?

Inhale.

A garbled moan leaves my lips as something carves a path through the three-foot-high grasses to my left. Before I can move, it's already out of earshot; gone, only the flattened trail any evidence it was there.

Exhale.

The encounter leaves me shaky but even more determined to carry on, knowing there may be more to this mountain than an urban legend, after all.

No way would he just leave. No way.

As I march off towards the haunting but beautiful harmony with even greater intent, my limbs feel fresh and rested—perhaps the adrenaline— but I suspect there's more to it. This place is like something from a fairy tale, colors more intense, sounds more crystal, and—holy crap—look at the size of that one! Stretching across four trees that loom ahead is a six-foot wall of webbing spanning perhaps a hundred feet.

Taking a wide berth, I cautiously march around the makeshift barrier, constantly scanning the long grasses for more signs of life. There's urgency in my movement now, this journey beginning to feel more than just a jaunt down memory lane. The floating soundtrack gets louder still, and I know I'm getting closer to its origin with every—

I arch my neck, squinting into the dullness in case my mind is playing tricks. That can't be.

About twenty feet to my right, staring directly at me from behind a cluster of rocks, is a human head. Our eyes lock. I try to speak, but there's not a drop of saliva in my mouth. Do I imagine this? Finally, I take a step forward, and the head snaps back behind the grey.

"Hey," I finally holler, launching myself towards the rocks, skipping over bushes, and dodging the boggier patches of mud. But I see nothing.

She was here. Right here!

Female, I'm sure of it, but not a hair on her head.

How did she get away so quickly? And what is she doing here? Is she alone?

"Hello!"

Silence.

As I scan the surroundings for signs of movement, I begin to see webs everywhere; huge sprawling tapestries that connect trees and sweep across rock formations. More than just the effect of reduced light, the atmosphere seems to be taking on an eerier tone; everything so still and quiet, even the breeze appears to have outstayed its welcome. The only sound on the mountain is that sweet melody, unmistakably female, a strange and seductive call that nourishes my inner core, filling me with excitement and—

Laughter. Faint, but coming from up there.

Even in the dull light, I can make out the crevice in the mountainside. At least, I think that's what it is, highlighted by the transition from grey to black. Approximately two hundred yards away and forty feet high in the rockface, it looks ominous but reachable.

As I begin to stride up the mountain, my adrenaline soars. I feel fear, but curiosity and excitement are winning. Something else, too; arousal. None of this makes sense, but the undeniable pull from that black hole is overpowering, and I know that I can't turn back now. I'm all in. The fragrance is becoming more intense, the music more beguiling, and I'm starting to feel lightheaded. The air seems thicker here, and for the first time, I'm getting tired—exhausted even—and I find myself wheezing, taking in huge mouthfuls of air. Things are no longer sharp. My footsteps are becoming heavier. More laughter floats across, but it's distorted and slow, as is the melody that continues to reel me in.

On the ground a few feet ahead, swimming in and out of focus, I see a carcass of sorts. It looks fake, unreal, but at the same time terrifying. That scuttling noise again, all around, but I can't see anything.

More laughing.

I reach out to the tree to steady myself, snapping my hand back as I feel more webbing crusting over my fingers. It's everywhere you look, walls of it, weaving in and out of the kaleidoscopic browns and greens that spin around me.

A nest?

The skeletal remains only add to the unease. A human skull attached to countless ribs with four legs on either side. My stomach drops. It's as though I'm floating, an out-of-body experience. I feel my left leg begin to buckle underneath me.

More human heads appear, some from within the cave, others behind rocks or trees, all completely hairless and female. Their eyes, though, so black, so alien, and their bodies—

It's too much.

As I slip down the side of the tree, I observe another of the creatures emerging from the hole. This one's bigger, and I instinctively know she's the maestro behind the music. Spindly legs jerk her forwards until her elongated and shiny black body is in full view. Grandly and menacingly, she begins her approach. Atop her head is a makeshift crown, an impressive weaving of twigs and grass that frames a face so stern and beautiful. Lips pursed together, her music continues to fill the mountain, and my body vibrates synchronously with the haunting undertone.

My arousal intensifies, but my skin crawls with simultaneous fear.

She turns her head towards me, and I see pincers in place of where the ears should be. Pedipalps—that's it—that's what my dad called them in the articles. Amazed by my recollection at such an intense moment, I can only watch, frozen to the spot as her glossy blackness menacingly draws in.

Whispering comes from all around. Movement too.

My stomach churns as she gets ever closer. I can see what appears to be a gland on the right side of her neck, wisps of green gas emerging from the glistening hole.

A sudden bolt of heat rushes across my left calf, and I snap my head around to find another human head smiling at me, huge black eyes and a large set of oversized fangs dripping with blood. Blackness spreads through my veins like an atlas of forbidden roads. Laughter surrounds me.

And this strange universe begins to wash away.

Jesus Christ, my head!

So dark, so cold. Where am I?

As my vision begins to adjust, I try and move, but something isn't right. My leg! No pink to be seen, just a blackened stump. "Help!" But only an ominous and distant dripping emerges from deeper within the cave.

I'm naked, suspended in air, at least three feet from the ground, my arms, and legs restrained by a colossal web that extends into darkness.

Those things. Hybrids of some sort, the stuff of nightmares.

I try and yank a hand free, but it's futile. This stuff is as strong as wire, cutting into my wrists.

"Help!"

And leaning against the side of the cave wall, I see it. No mistake. Nestled between an array of boots, flasks, and other paraphernalia that has no right being here is Father's backpack. Even after all these years, I'd recognize it anywhere.

The sight spurs me on, but as I struggle against the webbing, it cuts further into my wrists and legs. Come on! Come on! With gritted teeth and veins popping, I manage to break a couple of threads and let myself hope, but just as quickly, my stomach drops.

Tap-tap-tap. On the rock.

Something's coming.

Some *thing*.

Shadows move within shadows, whispers float. And there she is coming into view, the leader, the conductress, queen of the hybrids.

"Let me go!"

Others begin to rally around *her*, emerging from the darkness, scurrying across the rock walls, or scampering excitedly on the floor beneath. Some of them join me, gathering on the edge of the web.

"It will be over soon," *she* says. Her voice is clinical, the information delivered without emotion, devoid of human nuance. "We just need something you have."

I let out a shiver.

The first of the hybrids begins her approach towards me, eyes projecting only disdain. She bears her sinister fangs as she draws towards my crotch. "Don't flatter yourself," she says, turning around to show off her bulbous abdomen.

"We just need something you have," the leader repeats.

A humming begins, more intense than before. Coldness leaves, and soon my body tingles with warmth and writhes with unwanted pleasure against my silky constraints. I'm at once euphoric but full of fear. A heavy fog falls.

Thoughts of the backpack fade.

Thoughts of Jody fade.

Thoughts fade.

Instead, every sexual experience begins to simmer in my mind, every lustful urge, every licentious secret, until finally spilling over into a single extended montage of gratification. Louder and deeper to my core, the chorus goes. Images stretch beyond closed doors, heading towards the hidden recesses of carnality. More of that green gas cloaks me. And the hum. The hum. Stronger still, approaching a seemingly never-ending crescendo that—

Oh, God.

And just like that, I'm cold again. The hum fades, giving way to the distant dripping.

With pedipalps extended, the leader leans in and extracts my deposit. I watch, shivering as she carefully inserts it into the opening of the other's abdomen with the precision of a surgeon.

"You designed us," the leader says, "made us into what we are—genetically modified monsters. We hate you, but we need you."

It's too much to take in. Just another male that vanished from the face of the earth. "Why not mate with your own?"—a question I throw merely to slow down the inevitable ticking clock of death.

"Males are born without sexual glands. Humans designed them that way because they wanted to control us. They serve no purpose, so we kill them. It's just nature, or rather, part of our genetic programming. We need Human sperm to impregnate the female."

I shake my head, unable to process the insanity.

"You have no idea what else went on in that facility; humans are capable of unfathomable acts of cruelty and degradation." She averts her gaze to the floor. "Some managed to escape to this mountain, and here we still are—surviving, using a combination of sounds, scents, and pheromones to attract a human. It's controlled, infrequent, and just enough to maintain our species."

"My Father. He came here, too," I croak. "Jack. He had the red backpack over there."

She stops in her tracks and looks up towards me. Even with the cold black pebble eyes, I see a flicker of something register behind them. Effortlessly she continues her ascent, though, her first two legs planting

90

down either side of my waist.

Christ, is this it? Is this how I go?

Her face hovers directly above. "I birthed your father's children."

More hybrids join her, my feet now only inches from the floor as the web yields under the additional weight.

I look towards the pack for comfort, remembering some of the treats he used to bring out. Sometimes he'd even let me have a sip of whisky from his hip flask, and I would fake enjoyment but then cram my face full of chocolate as soon as he turned away.

I knew he hadn't deserted me. I knew it!

As I feel the first of the fangs sinking into my flesh, the thought gives me some consolation; that and the fact *our* legacy will continue, after all.

There's no magic here, only unfathomable depravity.

AUTHOR BIO

Mark Towse is an Englishman living in Australia. He would sell his soul to the devil or anyone buying if it meant he could write full-time. Alas, he began this journey late in life, penning his first story since primary school at the ripe old age of 45. Since then, he's been published in the likes of *Flash Fiction Magazine*, *The Dread Machine*, *Cosmic Horror*, *Suspense Magazine*, *ParABnormal*, and *Raconteur*, as well as over forty anthologies.

His work has also appeared on such exceptional podcasts as The Grey Rooms, No Sleep, Creepy, Chilling Tales for Dark Nights, and Tales to Terrify. His debut novella, *Nana*, was published earlier this year by D&T Publishing, and his recent novella, *Hope Wharf*, was just released. Be sure to stay tuned, as there are lots in the pipeline for the rest of 2021 and 2022!

THE CARRIAGE

BY N.E. SALMON

Ralph reread the text as another train thundered passed his platform at Liverpool Street Station. He didn't know how many times he had reread the same message, but each time he did, it seemed to lose meaning, as if his phone had switched to binary.

It was yet another apology letter from a possible employer. As the platform's florescent lights judged him, he tried, once more, to take in the words on the screen. He couldn't decide if this was a generic template they used where they just updated the *Insert Name Here* line with the candidate's name, but he was sure he hadn't gotten the job.

Sighing, he returned the phone to his pocket, ignoring its cries of low battery. He looked up at the platform terminal, cursing silently as "Delayed" scrolled slowly across its display.

Why did they even have that option? he thought sullenly. *That just gives me hope it might arrive. It should say either how long it will be or that the train has been canceled.*

He resisted the urge to kick the bag at his feet, even though it would assuage his boredom, and he knew there was nothing of value in there.

Resting his head against the back of the chair, he closed his eyes and listened to the electrified hum of the fluorescent lights.

It felt good to close his eyes, like a promise his terribly long day was finally ending. He was exhausted from a long day of job applications, followed by a failed job interview. He absently hoped he would be able to wake up early enough for work tomorrow, then ruthlessly remembered he didn't have a job anymore.

And I'll have to do it all again tomorrow, he thought.

In an unapologetic bluster of whistles, the train finally arrived and squealed to a stop in front of him. He quickly boarded, fell into the nearest seat, and let his bag tumble into the seat next to him. He checked the time on his dying phone, grimacing as it flashed 12:37 AM before fading to black.

It had taken longer than he had anticipated to pick up his things, despite them being thrown haphazardly into a corner. Claire had hovered over his shoulder the whole time, overseeing each item he packed. It didn't help that she would occasionally add something worthless to the pile or loudly proclaim whatever he was holding belonged to her.

At first, he had argued, but then realized it was pointless. They would go in circles each time as she claimed she'd bought the item or received it as a gift. After a handful of screaming matches, he decided it was easier to accept everything handed to or taken from him.

In the beginning, their relationship had been good, but when they finally decided to separate, it was as if they'd cleared the air of something that had been hanging over them for years. However, the stress of separating a life built together was quick to take its toll. Thankfully, the night was finally over. He had finally gathered the last of his belongings.

Without a phone to distract him, he stifled a yawn and looked out the window. The view was incredibly dull. Darkness enveloped the cool glass as the train trundled its way along the tracks, the occasional streetlight flashed passed in a distinct blur, and pale stations materialized and disappeared in a grim cycle of nearly identical images. Further, the carriage was empty.

Tales of ghost trains leapt into his mind, and he unconsciously hunkered down into his seat. The darkness from outside the window seemed to spread, surrounding him.

Don't sleep, he thought, feeling his consciousness slipping away.

"You've missed your stop," a calm voice said with a reassuring grasp of his shoulder.

Shit! Ralph awoke with a start, limbs flailing as he jumped out of his seat. The carriage was now bathed in light.

No, Ralph thought, filling with dread. *I couldn't have slept all night!*

Beside him stood a steward, his high-visibility vest shining like a small orange sun. He had blonde shoulder-length hair, and his blue eyes sparkled with humor that matched his broad smile. He seemed wearily accustomed to the occasional surprised visitor on his route.

"Sorry," Ralph said, retrieving his bag and placing it on his shoulders, "I must have overslept."

The steward sighed and sat down, rolling his eyes slightly before speaking.

"Too right, you overslept!" he replied, his smile twitching with slight exasperation. "You didn't even have the decency to snore so others would know you were here." The steward removed his satchel and, with a sigh, slammed it onto the seat next to him. "You've ruined a perfectly good trip."

Perplexed, Ralph continued to stare at the steward, watching as he rooted around in such a small bag for too long. The scraping of cloth filled the train as awkwardness stilled his tongue, though he wondered inwardly how a passenger could ruin a rail steward's trip. Indeed, they considered train journeys as both more trivial and severe than a trip, but never in between. The man's furrowed brow and thin smile showed that he was seriously aggrieved. It was not the scowl of, what Ralph imagined, was a slight inconvenience. The steward continued to root through his satchel, occasionally stopping at an unseen item before shaking his head. Ralph cleared his throat.

"I really am sorry. Truly. I'll get off at the next stop and pay whatever fine is needed." He considered adding another apology, but that would probably just annoy the steward, who was now running his hands through his hair.

"No. I'm the one who should be apologizing. I didn't check my surroundings when I Switched Tracks." The steward paused and looked out the window, allowing time for Ralph's rising confusion to fester into building panic. "If I let you off at the next stop, you wouldn't be able to get home. I don't mean it would be difficult; I mean it's impossible. You've managed, through no fault of your own and entirely by my doing, to leave the world that you know behind. I know it's difficult to believe what I'm telling you, but you must. The sooner we get through the disbelief, the better it will be for both of us. You've seen *The Wizard of Oz,* right? You're Dorothy. I'm the tornado." He waved lazily to the window.

Ralph didn't move. He *couldn't* move. Did the steward take pleasure in harassing confused passengers? Ralph didn't want to participate in the deteriorating mental condition of this man, but despite himself, he approached the window and squinted as his eyes adjusted to the bright light. Though, his mind would take much longer than his eyes to adjust.

Outside he saw a blue ocean that stretched to the horizon. The sparkling water rose to the submerged tracks, and waves lapped against the side of the train and sprayed the window. Ralph pressed his face against the glass, but the sunshine reflected off the steel train's sides and blinded him. The train heedlessly speeded forward. Ralph ran to the other side of the carriage and squished his palms and nose against another glass panel. Nothing but the ocean greeted him.

Once known as Mark Spencer, the steward attendant watched, trying not to smirk, as the man shook with denial, muttering, "it can't be" and "this is impossible." He still remembered his own reaction when he first slipped into another world.

The wails and screams will start soon, he thought.

Mark was frustrated, more at himself than anything. The fact remained that his vacation would have to be postponed until the drifter was seen safely home. If only he had searched the carriage before S*witching*. Then he'd already be on the way, halfway there to sunning himself on the triple sun-warmed beaches of Furngh.

Mark watched as the man sank to a fetal position on the ground between two rows of chairs. Mark peeled off his steward vest and thrust it into his satchel. He gathered Ralph into a nearby chair and sat down opposite him.

"Don't worry. That was the bad news. The good news is I can get you home. We'll have to pass through a few other carriages, and not all of them will be.... well.... familiar. But don't worry too much; they're mostly harmless. Just expect the unexpected. You're not in Kansas anymore," Mark chuckled to himself. The other man's head fell forward as though his forehead had tripled in weight.

"Can you do up this button for me?" the steward, Mark, said, holding out his arms, pointing with his chin to the back of his coat. Ralph had no idea where he had managed to get the calf-length, pale blue jacket but, as the coat was far too large to fit in the little satchel, Ralph guessed Mark had the coat hidden under one of the other seats. The jacket was adorned with leather lapels and golden buttons.

Ralph suddenly felt under-dressed. He looked down at his tattered and unkempt jacket, creased where he had slept in it. Ralph had thought he was smartly dressed from his interview, but now Mark's finery put him to shame. Regardless, he felt more in control of himself. He was on his way home, and that was what mattered.

97

Both this world and his own world back home moved on without him, ever-expanding. His small flat might as well be dust, its absence spinning slowly in an astral plane so far away he couldn't even fathom the distance. How or why had he come to this place? He would never find a satisfying answer, and the truth was, he didn't want to.

The buttons all fastened, Mark turned back to him, his hands once more rummaging in the Satchel at his side. *Had it always been that color?*

"Alright, your turn," Mark said, a smile still on his face. A pair of old boots, a tall fur hat, and a sleeveless fur vest appeared in his hands. Ralph decided, from now on, it was best he ignored the satchel. Silently, he took the items. Ralph removed his shoes, pointedly ignoring the holes in his socks, before quickly tugging on the calf-length boots. They slipped on easily, the black leather being surprisingly comfortable. He wore the rest of the strange outfit over his clothes.

"Good! Everything looks fine. Follow me," Mark nodded to himself and walked casually towards the doorway to the next carriage. The door opened with a hiss before he stepped through, one hand returning something into his satchel as he gestured for him to follow. Ralph looked away, intent on his resolution to ignore the pouch. He stepped forward, and the door snapped shut behind them.

Darkness covered them. Ralph blinked to adjust his eyes. Before him, he saw the small twitching flames of candles. Waxy smoke filled the carriage, and dozens of people filled the spaces. The carriage seats had been replaced with round tables and long lounging sofas. Each of the carriage's passengers was dressed in outstanding flattery. Long billowing dresses and tailored suits graced the causeways as couples danced to a jaunty piano number. They were standing in a giant ballroom, complete with a narrow dance way and a table laden with bottles and a heavy punch bowl. Ralph's nose burned with the odors of smoke and sweat. The swaying dancers and moving carriage shifted as though on the deck of a ship.

The dancers didn't notice their entrance. Some loungers nodded in their direction as though travelers from a different world were the norm.

Perhaps they are, Ralph thought as Mark nodded back. Luckily, while talking Ralph out of his panic, his more traveled friend had given him some tips on how best to approach what he might encounter. Unfortunately, Ralph had forgotten most of them, but he did remember one: *No matter what happens, don't ever tell anyone anything about your world. If anyone asks, just say you come from "up north" or "down south" and that the food there is amazing.*

Ralph's plan was simple; he would follow Mark Spencer and copy his behavior. Unfortunately, the plan was shattered when the piano ramped up, and Mark, along with all the other denizens, cheered and leapt onto the dance way, lapels and skirts twirling into a cloud of fabric. Abandoned and possibly the worst dancer in existence, Ralph meandered towards a drinks table, apologizing as he bumped into another table, causing its candle to spat at his disturbance. Avoiding eye contact with the candelabra, he quickly filled a silver cup with the punch and downed its contents. It tasted sweet and fruity and, more importantly, strongly of alcohol.

Then, he sat down on a lounge chair next to a happily chatting couple whose clothes and hair swapped shades in the candlelight. Ralph took another large gulp and stared at the dancers, his vision swimming with their fluid movements. Jealousy flared as he wondered how they could be so carefree when he was so far from home. In the darkness of the carriage, Ralph's mind filled with everything he had lost, the people he would never see again, the movies he had only seen the trailers for, the rent he wouldn't be able to pay....

Is that all I must lose? he thought, realizing the shallowness of his attachments.

"So where did you come from?" the lady next to him suddenly asked, her silver eyes dragging him out of his thoughts. He blinked at her slowly, scrambling to remember Mark Spencer's rules.

"The North. I'm from up North," he hoped he sounded more confident than he felt. "It's not so bad up there, all the food is perverted, but it does have terrifying beaches." He cursed to himself as he flubbed the line. The couple looked at him blankly for a moment, then smiled in synchrony.

"Ah yes, I've heard as such," the man said evenly, raising his cup to his lips. "Terribly good party today."

"For a Rosentho."

"Especially for a Rosentho!" They shared a giggle, and Ralph awkwardly joined in.

She tapped the man's arm reassuringly. "Though these tablecloths could certainly do with a bit more glamour!"

"Absolutely," Ralph nodded. "Though I will say the liquor more than makes up for the poor taste in tablecloths." They shared another giggle as he drained his cup. As the conversation moved towards the dancers, Ralph discovered he was enjoying himself. He realized if his tone remained in a pompous drone, he could say almost anything without reaction. Strangely, he didn't feel offended by their lack of interest. It was almost comforting just to sit there and talk at people who talked back at him.

He was persuaded to dance, which he should have known was a mistake, but the strange alcohol and cheery company swayed him. He realized it was the same song that had played earlier when he had lost Mark. He did his best to replicate the other dancer's twirls and leaps, hoping he didn't look as foolish as he felt.

The dancers twirled, fabric twisting, sweat glistening, and the liquid from their silvery cups spraying in alcoholic lassos around them. Songs merged, dances fused into a single motion, and even the occasional drunken tumble seemed choreographed. Around them, the carriage swayed and bucked in time with the music. Misted air swirled by the dancer's feet, a pirouetting storm flowing with them. The loungers lounged, the drinkers drank, and the dancers danced. They cried out as the song repeated yet again.

Exhausted, Ralph sank into a chair, too tired to refill his drink. The couple he was speaking with earlier reappeared at his side, sweat lightly misting their brows. Ralph loosened the top button of his shirt and removed his hat.

"Where are you from?" the lady asked again. Silver hair shadowed her face.

"The south," Ralph replied absently. The man and woman each smirked at him.

"Ah yes! I remember," the man said, spilling some of his drink on himself as he took a sip from his glass. "Incredible ball they've thrown tonight, isn't it?"

"For a Rosentho," the lady mocked.

"Yes, yes," Ralph said, setting his glass down on the table. "I just wish the pianist would play a different song. We've heard this song a dozen times now."

"I'm sorry? The man asked, a large, purple stain growing on his shirt.

"Where is the pianist? Or is this a recording?"

"What are you talking about?" the man's voice had a sharpened edge.

"The music," Ralph asked. "Where is it coming from?"

Men and women in the surrounding area suddenly stopped and turned to stare at Ralph, their eyes red and dry. Oblivious, Ralph waved his hands in poor mimicry of a conductor.

"Surely it must change sometime," Ralph insisted. "You can't listen to the same song on repeat for eternity!"

The entire room fell to silence.

"Why would you want change?" asked the man with the stained shirt. Then the man leaned forward, and the pungent odor of spirits on his breath instantly sobered Ralph. "Where did you say you came from?"

'The N-north?" Ralph stammered.

"Where in the North, exactly? How did you get here?" the man asked, stepping forward.

The other partygoers crowded in from all sides, and Ralph noticed the music had stopped. Ralph stumbled out of his chair and began backing away towards the door he'd come from, but the mob followed him. Then a pale, robed figure jumped out, causing Ralph to yelp in surprise.

"Time to go!" the figure chirped. It was Mark Spencer, grinning slyly from underneath the hood of his robes. Mark spun Ralph around and urged him forward, quickly. The crowd erupted, shouts echoing around the carriage as Mark deftly led Ralph in a twirling ballet through the crowd. Bottles smashed around them, and a candelabra fell with a crash as they finally reached a door.

"Wait for me," Mark said, still grinning as he pushed Ralph through the door. Ralph tried to protest, but the door shut with a loud metal bank, leaving him stunned.

What had been a pale wooden door was now a wrought iron hatch with a large rusty wheel in place of a door handle. The door now appeared more suitable for a submarine than a ballroom.

Ralph sank to the ground, noticing for the first time that the floor was lush green grass. Steeling himself, he turned around, surprise mixing with fear as he saw the looming forest in front of him, a curved bow of trees on each side of a small corridor. Above him, a small amount of sunlight filtered through. It was a welcome sight after the candlelit dimness of the last carriage.

Feeling cold now, he re-buttoned his borrowed vest, his mind trying to come to terms with recent events. He brushed his hand over his face, realizing too late that it was now heavy with dew. He wiped his face, now wet and smelling of earth, on his sleeve. All the while, his eyes never left the tree line. It was making him paranoid.

102

What if those people come for me?

He could imagine them bursting open the door behind him, carrying pink Molotov cocktails and silver pitchforks. He shivered.

"Mark would understand," he said, stepping into the woods.

Twenty minutes later, he realized he was lost. He wandered until he found a tree which he thought he recognized, but it only led to an unfamiliar clearing.

The smell of wood smoke tingled in his nostrils as he spotted some huts perched on a hill. Hesitant but curious, he approached the nearest cabin and cleared his throat loudly. A loud grunt responded, then Ralph's eyes grew large.

Unfortunately, he was too slow to dive for cover, and he was left staring up at a creature that stood two feet taller than him. It had a heavy stoop and low-hung head perched above a long-pelted robe that trailed on the ground around it. A large snout protruded from the hood of the robe. He wouldn't have noticed the robe if it hadn't been for the black kitchen knife-shaped claws that quivered gently at the end of the creature's long arms on either side. At first, the creature's large cat-like green eyes stared blankly over Ralph's head, the thin, black lips glistening as the creature flicked its tongue between them.

Ralph stood frozen to the ground, his mind screaming to flee, but his hands trembling and his legs unmovable. His bladder suddenly felt full, and his breath burned, trapped in his lungs.

The creature twitched and looked down onto Ralph, who closed his tear-filled eyes, readying himself for death.

"I'm sorry," the creature said, its voice surprisingly high-pitched. "I hadn't expected visitors, or I would have tidied up."

Mark Spencer had begun to worry. He'd been searching for too long now and was running out of time. Suddenly, he remembered a drink spilled on

103

him near one of the punch bowls and hastened towards it. Everyone ignored him as he strolled through the ball.

This is the problem with these guys, he thought, looking under a table. *If something doesn't match their worldview, it's either a threat, or it's invisible.*

"Ah-a!" He screamed in triumph, sweeping aside some empty bottles, and holding up his little silver flask, thumbs lovingly tracing its edges.

"Couldn't leave without this!" he chirped to a couple nearby. They shifted uneasily before turning their backs.

Just as expected, Mark thought with a chuckle as he stepped out of the door he'd pushed Ralph through.

Pastora.

He'd always loved coming here. Though a bit on the dull side, he had fond memories of camping in the Never-Ending Woods. Moreso, the ale brewed here was cheap and strong. Noticing Ralph wasn't anywhere to be seen, Mark rolled his eyes. Luckily, there weren't many places he could've gone from there.

Mark decided to make his way to the nearest resort. He wondered what it was that made Pastorans so happy to talk to travelers. Usually, a world would try to reject its visitors, yet Pastora welcomed everyone with open arms. Maybe it was their lack of leadership. With no one trying to rule over anyone else, they were under no pressure to avoid anybody else. Within minutes, he heard laughing and the low tones of conversation coming from a nearby clearing. Siling, he approached the nearest hut.

Inside, Ralph was laughing and looking ridiculous in an oversized chair, and a smiling Pastoran doubled over in laughter, struggling to keep hold of a large cup of tea clutched between its claws.

"What's the joke?" Mark asked, sitting on the armrest of an empty chair. Ralph wiped a tear from his eye, and the Pastoran looked over.

"Hello, friend! Ralph was just telling me about...what was it called?"

104

"Job Interviews," Ralf said, shifting uncomfortably. "I was explaining what I was doing before I met you, and she found the concept of an Interview amusing. Then, for some reason, I started to find it funny too! Especially when she explained how they do it here."

"We just get given a job at birth, and we do it. It's effortless. Why would you need to do otherwise?" Ralph snorted, and the Pastoran, still shocked, shrugged and laughed. Mark chuckled and stood up.

"Right, time to go," mark hopped up from the chair, then both Mark and Ralph bid farewell to their host. Once they had bid goodbye, Mark led them towards the next switch.

"So, how do you like Pastora?" Mark asked.

"Scary at first, but I grew to like it."

"Yes, it is very nice here. Many people choose to travel here for the holidays." Mark refrained from adding *to get drunk cheaply.* "But in general, they visit because the Pastorans are always welcoming."

"She *was* friendly."

They walked through dense undergrowth on a narrow dirt path. The sky darkened, the overhead branches knotted into a thick ceiling, and on each side, the trunks solidified with moss and vines. The sounds of the forest grew louder, the creaks of trees transformed into a crescendo, thickening into a sound like the rolling of a train track. At the end of the tunnel, a wall of vines twisted into the shape of a crude door.

Mark stopped. In his hand, he held a spherical metal object. "Here we are," he said, still smiling. "Home at last."

Ralph looked at the door with a touch of sadness that he couldn't explain. Now that he was here, he didn't want to leave. Mark must have noticed his sorrow, for he placed a comforting hand on his shoulder, then began shuffling through his satchel until he found a tiny piece of paper with a few numbers on it.

"This is my number," he said uneasily, having never done something like this before. "Call me if you ever want to travel the worlds again."

"I will!" Ralph enthused, quickly taking it. Then with puzzlement, he said, "There are only four numbers here. What's this line for?"

"Last Call," Mark said, pressing a button on the sphere in his hand, which caused the vine door to slither open.

Mark waved and walked onto the next carriage, his hand once more in his satchel as he disappeared into another world on another adventure. Left alone, Ralph stared at the clock above. The train had turned into Liverpool Street several days earlier.

Ralph looked again at the piece of paper Mark had given him but couldn't make sense of it. Sighing, he looked at his phone, surprised but not shocked that it had somehow recharged and that the date remained the same as when he left. More miraculously, however, he seemed to have an unread message.

Ralph looked at it and smiled. Stuffing Mark's number in his pocket, he began typing a reply. As he heard the rattling of an approaching train, Ralph knew his life had forever changed.

AUTHOR BIO

N.E. Salmon is a London-born writer whose primary skill is falling asleep in any and every situation. When he is not napping, he is irregularly updating his blog at TheSalmonMuse.wordpress.com and debating the causes and consequences of fantasy plot points with himself and his less fantasy-oriented but politely attentive wife. Since receiving his joint honors degree in English Literature and History, N.E. Salmon has begun work on a science fiction novel, the editing of which has also been set aside to work on more short stories and plans for newer, more exciting, less edited novel ideas.

ATA NOR

BY MICHAEL A WEXLER

The blackness of the forest stretched unbounded.

The night had fallen warm and humid. My skin glistened with moisture, causing my hair to hang in my eyes. I gripped my sword and moved blindly forward through a sodden world, dark and unwelcoming—a silent world of spongy earth and soggy leaf mold. Even the trodden twigs beneath my leather boots were too damp to crack.

Soon enough, I would find a light at the fiery pit of the great beast, Ata Nor.

My way led through rough brush and tall trees that were crowded, cramped, and devoid of life. Nothing dared live in the domain of Ata Nor. Yet, I fretted over fanciful evils I knew did not exist. I heard padded footfalls born in my imagination, threatening my every step.

At once, I halted, squaring my shoulders, and shaking my head. A forced growl sent them scattering back to my overwrought subconscious. Was there not enough to challenge my courage in the nearness of Ata Nor? Need I further burden myself with ghosts and phantoms?

I took up the trail again. Faint and first and then growing ever stronger, the noxious waft of poisonous vapors touched my searching nostrils—spewed from the bottomless pit that was home to the faceless demon Ata Nor.

There was nothing supernatural or imaginary in the rush of heat that soon closed about me, stinging my flesh and eyes. Even at a distance, I felt a presence of evil, a taste of death. I paused, listening. Did Ata Nor cry out, or was it only the wind? Or, as the ancient ones proclaimed, the wailing spirits of the lost souls already fallen into the pit and devoured by the endless blood lust of the final conqueror, Ata Nor.

I had reached an exceptionally thick and bending part of the forest. The gases flung from the pit of Ata Nor descended thick and choking, the heavy canopy of blackened treetops prohibitive of any escape. I forced my lips to clamp against the acrid fumes, yet they seeped into me like serpents sent to strangle and kill.

A curve in the forest bent the now billowing smoke beyond my vision, and in that smoke, I suddenly saw the unholy vanguard of Ata Nor. The smoke rose and took shape, becoming as naked sirens calling, coaxing, fairly daring me to press on. Their voices were a low, throaty humming that pulled at me. I wondered how any man could resist.

My nerves strained; my muscles flexed. Irrationally, I sent my great sword slicing through the incorporeal images. They laughed, unaffected, for they were not real.

Again, the low growl of an angry beast escaped my parched throat, and the crisis passed. My blood ran hot again. I had allowed myself to fall into the trap of imagination. Was it my failing or simply the tried and proven torture that Ata Nor wrought upon each of his victims?

The answer may have sat as nebulous as the smoke-shrouded forest, but for one fact: I was not as any who had gone before. *I am a warrior.* I was a man amongst children. I did not shrink from fairy tales and childish make-believe, nor did I fear the dark or the unknown. Instead, I stood tall, braced for combat, equal to the trial ahead.

Of all the men in the village, I had been chosen to end the reign of Ata Nor. I alone dared to do so.

I remembered old Basamet, his sitting with me on the hour before my departure. How many years had Basamet been tribal elder? It appears he had been gray and withered since I was pink and suckling at my mother's breast. But his eyes never lost the glow of youth. Even in old age, his eyes sparkled so much that the whiteness of his beard seemed absurd. It seemed as if his beard should be just as black and youthful as his eyes.

"You go upon the noblest of missions," he said.

"Is that just another word for dangerous?" I asked.

There came a sudden darkening to Basamet's countenance. The sparkle turned cold with candidness.

"I have sat as we sit many times in my lifetime," he said in slow, measured words. "Each time, I sat and spoke with the chosen warrior, as I do now. Sadly, each meeting had just been a prelude to death. Yet, every brave man had been confident they would succeed where the others had failed. Is it not the same with you?"

"Could it be another way? If the wolf feared its prey, it would starve."

"You have the power of youth," he said, "as did all those before you. You were an easy choice, as you have often demonstrated your skill in the hunt and won many of the contests of strength. But this journey is to the pit of Ata Nor...."

"It is different," I replied.

Basamet nodded.

"With triumph, you'll become the greatest warrior ever to stride Earth. But if you fail...."

"Fail, and I am but one in a line of boastful pretenders."

"Fail, and you are dead and soon forgotten. It will become taboo even to speak your name because the mere speaking of it will be a reminder of the unholy power of Ata Nor."

I smiled at Basamet and said, "I shall return in triumph. Ata Nor will be defeated and our people free of his bloodlust. I shall accomplish all of this, Ancient One."

"If you live."

"I shall live."

So, it was I went forward with sharpened sword and ready dagger, leading a celebratory procession to the edge of the black and dismal forest. I watched as the cheering crowd withdrew, quietly, quickly, shrinking from view, their terror of these woods and what lurked within written keenly upon their war-weary faces. It was a war not of man against man but man against the unnatural man against the faceless demon, Ata Nor.

I had set forth upon my quest in a strident mood. My confidence was bolstered by the youth's vigor and the will of an unbeaten warrior. A poise soon sobered by the bleak reality of the lonely wood, the heavy boughs hanging close above, the looping vines requiring constant avoidance, and the rich stink of the unseen pit of the beast.

Eventually, I saw the faint glow of the fire, and the pit's vaporous mist became visible in the dark. The full measure of my youthful bluster returned at the sight.

Ata Nor drew close, and I welcomed him.

A welcoming that quickly transformed into a new and pressing concern. The fog thickened. What began a gentle breeze now blew strong like flying wraiths blowing hotly across my brow. I wiped at my sweat and dried my hands on the nearest tree to better grip my sword.

The trees thinned. I could see the beginnings of a glade, an open space of fifty yards at the edge of which sat a yawning pit of shimmering flame. I had found the burning home of Ata Nor.

The legends were true, for I confess to my previous doubts.

As old Basamet had lamented, in the memory of man, no human

111

foot ever come this far was known to return. No eye of man had ever seen the great beast and lived to recall the beast's face or voice. Even the oldest of the village folk could not prepare me for what I might meet. All any of the villagers knew was how, in the depth of darkest night or by the light of the brightest sun, Ata Nor would come, invisible and irresistible, to carry away another victim. His gluttonous appetite from human flesh ever and anon stealing a life, leaving a bereaved and shattered community behind. Ata Nor picked no favorites. Man, woman, and child all succumbed; young, old, hero, and coward, for is not humanity full of each? Yet seemingly never enough to satiate his implacable hunger.

Ata Nor came, silent and soundless, and someone died certain as the grieving that followed.

Sight of the great flaming hole in the earth flooded within me a sudden and unfamiliar hesitancy. I had battled the beasts of the fields and the men of the valley. None had taken the better of me, never had I hesitated. Those victories had created within me a fearsome warrior, the best of the best—the one chosen to vanquish Ata Nor. Yet, I faltered. Was this fear? If so, I felt no different. Perhaps I only grew more cautious, more calculating of an unknown enemy. Yes, that was it. Caution. Not the foolishness of the village elders who warned that I advanced against the devil himself.

"To think that," I cried aloud, "one must also believe in Gods. I accepted neither." I raised my sword hand high. "My faith lies in my blade."

Shoulder's squared, hesitation cast aside, I advanced. My feet felt possessed with their own intent. Clearing the forest, I stepped quickly into the shadows. The only light came from the gaping pit of fire. I smiled. I sensed no unholy demon, no supernatural being. I crept forward to the very edge of the abyss, leaning forward as far the inferno permitted, fighting searing heat, looking, searching. I saw nothing, only the fanning flames falling away forever.

"Ata Nor!" I cried boldly. "Come forward, face me, and we shall

112

learn which is the greater force: good or evil."

A few loose boulders lay nearby. I hefted one and heaved it into the pit. It disappeared with a hissing noise, not unlike an angry serpent. I waited. Ata Nor deigned not to respond. I wondered, was it possible he had vacated his ghastly hole and was now abroad seeking fresh prey?

Perhaps. It mattered not at all. I would wait for Ata Nor until the first rays of dawn, whereupon I would return to my hut and tell my tale. I would beguile the women and children, and I would bask before the warriors. Then sleep, venturing out upon the morrow and every morrow thereafter until the deed was done.

Surrendered to the intense heat, I backed away from the pit's edge. Again, the foggy mist enveloped me. It seemed deeper and wetter than before. Or was it just I had not realized how badly I perspired from my nearness to the flames? I cursed quietly and sought to cool myself by reentering a small, uncluttered plot of the forest. But the mists pursued me. A heavy cloud of vapor now laden with bits of ash came at me. It became impossible to escape lest I retreat entirely from the wood, which I would not do. I vowed to hold my ground.

"I should conserve my strength," I mused aloud, for suddenly, I felt weary. It came upon me without warning and caused my knees to buckle. With a low snarl, I took to sit cross-legged upon the forest floor, my great sword resting upon my knees—the sudden slack in my vitality a puzzlement.

An unwelcome stab of pain in my ribs caused my thoughts to harken to a recent battle with the Valley tribe. I had killed a dozen men. There had been fleeing terror at my ferocity and the ferocity of my tribe. I touched at my right side, where a sword had penetrated me. It had been a deep wound, but it was no worse than a dozen such injuries I'd endured in past skirmishes.

I grew sleepy. A long overdue breeze rose. It was pleasant, and it pleased me with its caress. Upon its breath, it carried strange new scents:

113

flowers laden with memories of forgotten places, worlds of my youth, and conquests.

A strange sense swept over me, a sudden realization I had seen so very much in my young life, known so many faces and souls, and yet, I was alone. I had always been alone. And what kind of life had that loneliness wrought?

Was there love? I had known the company of women far and wide, but I'd never known love. There was never one beauty above another. Was there hate? I had warred often and killed many men. Did I hate them? Did I know a single soul long enough or well enough even to care if they died? No, and indeed I slew without hate. I slew from duty and the blind hatred others forced upon me.

I saw figures upon the breeze: men running carrying swords, racing along a line of destiny that ran back to my earliest days. It was as if a door had opened upon my entire existence, and it thew forth every life I had connected and affected.

Across that door hung a filmy curtain against which the wind blew to the effect of a gutted candle. I heard a murmur of voices that sought to council and console me. But of what? I felt no guilt. I did not create the wars I fought in; such is the fate of those sworn to duty.

Duty or slavery?

With a start, I awoke, my head filled with questions. With an effort, I rose to my feet, hoping to cast aside my sordid dream, but then I saw it. No-not *It*. I saw *her*.

I gasped in shock, but you must forgive my surprise at the sight. For in the center of the small space, the swirling mists had congealed into a solid form. Though more haze than stone, it shimmered with life. It was a human figure, a woman to be precise-a woman so beautiful it was beyond conception. And she was inching towards me. This naked, vaporous entity, for it could not be real, stretched her arms to wrap me and draw me close. I saw nails of great length, stained crimson, and tipped with fire.

Impossible.

The thing's eyes were lit and sparking, flushing her cheeks, and highlighting curved lips burned with crimson and tinted orange, blue and black.

I would not allow this illusion. At once, I proclaimed it a trick of Ata Nor. No.... this *was* Ata Nor! The demon was casting an enchantment to disarm and make me vulnerable. I would not have it.

I swung my sword upwards, slicing through the mirage. The air moved, the flames rippled and danced, but the illusion remained. A tinkling of laughter joined the crackling of the blaze.

"You will not possess me, Ata Nor!" I cried, forced to retreat two steps. "Show yourself in your true form. My sword awaits."

Now, oddly, unexpectedly, the fiery figure ceased dancing. The well of flame from which Ata Nor had surely emerged had dimmed, cooled. Could it be that it iced? Awed, I stood, peering into the incalculable depth of mist and darkness surrounding me. Suddenly, from the very heart of the specter, there came a voice.

"It is time, Great Warrior."

The woman returned, smiling. By instinct, my sword struck out, carving through her form, which was not mist at all but solid flesh, bone, blood, and muscle. As real as I. My cut rose upward and then veered sideways through a white and enticing neck that sparkled with pearly dew. And when that mighty blade again found air, the naked figure of Ata Nor stood as before. No blood, no injury, no change.

"There is no need to strike out so," sang the phantom. "Embrace me, for is that not the journey's end you seek? Come, fear not. Your struggles end here, Brave Warrior. You have but to nestle against my breast, and all shall be as it is ordained to be."

"I ordain who and what shall be my struggles. I embrace only the victory of today and the challenge of tomorrow. And this victory shall be the death of you, Ata Nor."

In reply, the vision laughed and flowed forward as if cast upon a vast wind. She fully engulfed me, and though I pushed hard against the waif, I could not move. Lethargy returned twice-fold. My chest burned; my limbs trembled. I dropped my sword.

Ata Nor softened and became a palpably lithe and subtle woman, lovely beyond description. I lost all fear and felt only a sudden, overwhelming desire to surrender. I gazed upward. The first faint rays of the sun smiled down upon us. Clouds moved apart, and a piece of heaven opened. My eyes watered with the first dew of the day.

The beckoning morning called me as nothing had called to me before.

In the arms of Ata Nor, I began to rise. The tiredness fled. The pain of all my wounds, earned over a lifetime of war, evaporated. Great peace come upon my being, contentment I had never known before.

As we rose, I gazed back down into the still shadowed forest, and there I saw not an empty wood but an open plain, sunbathed and littered with the remains of a great battle. There too was the flaming hole of Ata Nor, filled with flailing corpses. I looked upon both sides of death.

A vague remembrance crowded my mind a flash of crashing bodies and banging swords, of flying knives, and of grunting screaming men. I understood. There was nothing to fear from Ata Nor. The beast of the pit would not rise for me. I should never see or know his clutching hands.

I flew with an angel.

Indeed, my struggles had come to an end. A far greater power had judged me and rendered a decision.

I felt sad for my friends and family, as they did not know the beauty and tenderness that could be theirs, if only they could find the wisdom to live in peace. I felt everlasting pity for the doomed souls that had caused the great battle from which I had been lifted, for when their time came, they would know Ata Nor.

Basamet would go here, in the great flaming pit of Hell.

I allowed myself to go limp, nestled to my angel's breast. I could feel the beat of her heart, loud and strong, as my own heartbeat slowed, faded, and stopped.

AUTHOR BIO

Born and raised in Philadelphia, Michael Wexler, an accomplished guitarist, had an exciting and enriching musical youth and was privileged to work with many famous personalities, including Jimi Hendrix, Ike and Tina Turner, Chuck Berry, and others. Always interested in writing, he began putting his creative juices to work as a part-time ghostwriter and editor before eventually settling into a fulfilling career as a graphic designer. Those successes have allowed Michael to write novels and short stories full-time in the Pulp Detective, Horror, and Heroic-Fantasy genres.

To read Michael's recently published Hard-Boiled story, "Mona's Back" in *Pulp Adventures # 36*, visit BoldVenturePress.com/pulp-adventures-36

HER MUSE

BY KAY HANIFEN

To love the fae is to invite madness. To them, we are moonflowers—delicate and blooming in one night before fading into eternity. We're hardly worth the effort to them most of the time, but some fae consider us more than toys. Some even find love in humans, but this can be just as deadly as bringing their ire upon you.

I don't pretend to be a great writer and artist, I'm mediocre at best, but it doesn't stop me from pursuing my true great love. I can sit for hours drawing whatever inspires me and write the night away when the world is quiet, and I'm the only one awake. It was a cool, early autumn day when I first met her. I'd gone to the park with my sketchbook and music to lose myself in the meditative work of capturing an image on a page.

As I sat at a picnic table with my colored pencils, my eyes were drawn to the most beautiful woman I'd ever seen. Her hair was as fiery as the trees, and its shifting in the gentle breeze reminded me of the movement of flames in a hearth. Her facial proportions reminded me of a China doll—so perfect that they could only have been painted on. She sat beneath a tree, staring up at the soft clouds in the bright blue sky, her full lips curled into a faint smile. She must've noticed me staring because her bright green eyes met mine, and she arched a perfect eyebrow.

I blushed and looked down, only to realize that I'd been unconsciously drawing her while I stared. I'd done exercises where I'd draw a face without looking. They were always wonky and disproportionate, resembling a Picasso more than a human being. This, though, looked almost like I'd done it on purpose.

"Is that supposed to be me?" a voice asked from behind, making me jump. It was high and feminine with a musical quality that told me she could be a professional opera singer if she wanted.

Startled, I whipped around and locked eyes with the beautiful woman. "Oh, sorry. I didn't realize I was—I mean, it was an accident. I can scrap it if you want."

"You did that by accident," she said, sitting down across from me with an enchanting smile, "I'd like to see what you can do on purpose."

That afternoon, I drew something far beyond my talents. Her portrait was almost lifelike as I strove to capture every perfectly placed hair and the glint of humor in her eyes. It was near dark when I blinked and looked up from my sketchbook. Somehow, I'd spent hours drawing this stranger and hadn't even noticed. "Sorry if I kept you here," I said, and she waved dismissively.

"Nonsense. You have talent. Meet me here at the same time tomorrow." She got to her feet and did something I didn't expect; she cupped my cheek in her silky soft hands. "I look forward to seeing you again."

"Wait," I said as she disappeared into the forest, "I don't know your name."

She paused at the tree line, looking over her shoulder with a warm smile. "Call me Leah."

"I'm Rosaline," I replied, but she'd vanished.

That night, I couldn't get her out of my head. Every time I closed my eyes, I saw that red, cupid's bow smile and green catlike eyes. After tossing and turning for hours, I pulled out my laptop and began to write. My fingers flew across the keyboard as I wrote poems, short stories, and even the first few chapters of a novel. I was used to bursts of creativity at night, but this was unlike anything I'd ever felt before. My mind felt afire with ideas, and my fingers couldn't seem to catch up.

The sun was high in the sky when I came out of my trance. The needs of my body made themselves known as soon as I closed out of the word document. Somehow, it was three o'clock in the afternoon. My eyelids felt heavy from the lack of sleep, my hunger had grown into nausea, and I had to run to the toilet to make it in time.

And yet, I felt refreshed and energized, as though I'd gotten a full night's rest. After a quick meal, I changed out of my clothes and returned to the park in the hope of seeing Leah again. This time, I brought along my notebook as well in case I wanted to write some poetry.

She sat at the same table as the day before, her hair braided intricately and wearing a soft-looking sweater. Leah smiled when she saw me, and my body felt as though someone had run an electric current through it. I've never been one for sex but seeing her, I began to understand how those who experience attraction must feel all the time.

"How was your night?" she asked with a smile that seemed to indicate that she already knew how it had gone.

"Surprisingly productive," I said, sitting down across from her. I pulled out two honey-crisp apples I'd brought with me. I bought them the other day from my favorite stand from the farmer's market. They always tasted perfect, with a balance of sweet and tart that made it versatile for eating plain, baking, or making cider. I offered one to her and took the other for myself. Leah narrowed her eyes at me and looked so suspicious that I couldn't help but laugh.

"Oh, you caught me. I poisoned that apple so I could be the fairest in the land."

Her stare turned into confusion. "I didn't think you had tampered with it, but...."

"I didn't!" I said quickly, "it was a bad joke. Sorry."

Slowly, she lifted the apple to her lips and took a bite. Her eyes closed in pleasure at the taste. "A worthy offering."

If I thought it was a strange thing for her to say at the time, I didn't mention it. While she delicately ate the apple, I sketched the angles of her face, shading the red of her hair the same color as that of the apple. Over several hours, I filled my sketchbook with art and poems, only stopping when I reached the last page. Like yesterday, I looked up only to realize that it was full dark. Somehow, I hadn't noticed the sunset or the growing chill. My hand cramped, my eyes burned, and just about every bodily need I'd neglected in the past several hours made themselves known again.

Leah sat across from me, watching me with a faint smile. She slid the book closer to herself, examining the art and poems like a detective searching for an answer to a mystery.

"These are quite good," she said, "have you considered publishing your writing or submitting your art to a gallery?"

Honestly, I hadn't. Art, to me, was a release. It didn't matter to me that I wasn't the next Michelangelo or Charles Dickens. Greatness was never my destiny, and I made peace with it long ago. But these were good—better than I'd ever done before. Maybe I did have some potential.

With inhuman grace, she crossed the picnic table so that she stood next to me. Wordlessly, she tipped my head up, pressing a gentle kiss to my lips. Kissing her was like kissing gentle springtime, her lips warm like the sun and soft like flower petals. The parting of our lips left me dizzy and aching for more. I wanted nothing more than to bury myself in her, to inhale her sweet, floral scent and run my fingers through her flaming locks. But, like yesterday, she departed again with a request that I see her tomorrow.

The following day I had work but spending the afternoon with Leah was infinitely more important. I toiled the night away, sending out my art and writing to any publisher I could find. For weeks, I barely slept or ate, and I neglected my job in favor of making both art and love to Leah.

I should have known something was off about her. She was a shambling pile of red flags hidden behind a too-perfect face, but let's be honest, no one's first guess would be that she's fae. It's unlikely to be their second guess either. And even if I had known, I probably wouldn't have cared because the inspiration she gave me was an addiction. I'd struggled occasionally with writer's and art block, trying desperately to find a muse to get me through my latest project, but after meeting Leah, I felt like a fountain overflowing with ideas. Neither hunger nor sleep touched me while I created the most beautiful art I'd seen in my life and sent it out to whoever would take it. Within two months, I no longer worried about being fired from my job. I was making enough money as an artist to sustain myself.

Leah moved in after three months. Having her in such close proximity transformed my overflow of inspiration into a tsunami. I don't believe I slept or ate for a week straight after she first arrived. Sometimes, she would try to tear me away from my work, but I had a novel to write, a graphic novel to illustrate, and a cacophony of ideas in my head.

And then, a local gallery offered to display my work at an upcoming gala. Though I'd barely stepped out of the house the past few months, I knew I had to go. Maybe I was cut out for the art scene after all.

On the night of the gallery, I stood in front of my mirror, Leah braiding my long, neglected hair and pinning it up with silver. For the first time in a long time, I found myself staring in the mirror, but I didn't recognize the woman across from me. I'd lost weight over the past few months. I've always been on the heavier side, so people would probably congratulate me on that. But the dark, bruise-like bags under my eyes were another story. How much *had* I been sleeping? I honestly couldn't remember the last time I'd gone to bed on purpose instead of passing out in front of my laptop or at my easel.

"The all-seeing sun ne'er saw you match since first the world begun," Leah said, pressing the final pin in place and then a kiss to my forehead, "My fair, fair Rosaline."

I giggled like a schoolgirl, my face burning even after months of living with a flirt like her. "What did the Rosalind from that other play say? Love is merely madness and, I tell you, deserves a dark house as well and a whip as madmen do, and the reason why they are not so punished and cured is that the lunacy is so ordinary that the whippers are in love, too."

A strange look crossed Leah's face at that quote. I was about to apologize for upsetting her somehow when she smiled and tucked a stray lock of hair behind my ear. "I knew you were special from the moment I first saw you that autumn afternoon. Your talent was like coal, ready to be pressed into a diamond if you had enough drive and passion. And now you and your art are the stars of this gala."

"Well, I had a very inspiring muse," I said, pressing a dizzying kiss to her soft lips. Or maybe I was just dizzy. I stood up too fast and staggered, leaning against the bathroom sink. She grabbed me by my arms with a cry of concern and led me to the bed so I could sit down. While I blinked the two Leah's into one, she bit her lips and paced back and forth.

"Perhaps you should rest tonight. I don't suppose you've eaten," she said.

I gave her a tired smile and took her hand mid-stride. "I'm fine. It's just a dizzy spell."

"That's how it always begins," she said, eyes glistening with tears that sparkled like diamonds.

I opened my mouth to ask what she meant but was interrupted by a call from the gala manager asking me how long it would be before we arrived. "We're on our way out now," I told him.

When we arrived, it felt like I'd stepped into a fairytale. Women in glittering ball gowns danced alongside men in handsome tuxedoes. Leah plied me with hors-d'oeuvres and drinks.

I remember that night in snapshots: a pale hand holding a champagne flute, an older man laughing among a group of other older men, Leah's smile as she took in the oil painting that I'd completed just a month ago. The picture was an intimate moment of her getting out of bed, silk nightgown askew. She had her back to the viewer but looked over her shoulder with a warm smile on her lips and mussed hair. The room was bathed in the gentle glow of morning, and there were pillow creases on her cheek from a night of heavy sleeping. Despite the messy hair and the creased cheek, she was still breathtaking. That one was my favorite. It captured the warmth and comfort I felt waking every morning beside her. Leah stared at it with a soft sort of sadness that made her look far older than her years.

I placed my hand on her shoulder. "Are you okay?"

She nodded absently. "Is this truly how you see me? I look so.... human."

"Well, yeah. You're the most beautiful person I'd ever met, but you're still a person. Love isn't just found in the pretty moments. It's in the mundane and the ugly, and I wanted to capture how an ordinary morning with you felt like magic."

"You are such a romantic," she said, pressing a kiss to my forehead. It held a strange warmth that trickled down my face and the rest of my body, "My love, may you keep creating art for as long as you live." Her words held power to them that sent a shiver down my spine. I blinked, my vision blurring and my knees buckling. She helped me to a chair and cupped my cheek, the warmth seeping into my bones. And suddenly, I had a thousand ideas I needed to get down. My thumbs were a blur on my phone as I typed it all in the notes app. I hardly noticed her pull me to my feet and lead me out to a taxi.

She was gone the following day, but I hadn't noticed. I'd spent the whole night writing and drawing until my hands cramped, and I passed out at the table. Somewhere in my mind, buried beneath ideas for poems, paintings, and novels, I knew something was deeply wrong. I couldn't stop even if I wanted to. Even as I forced myself to get to my feet and eat something, I typed lines of dialogue and snippets of poetry in the notes section of my phone, and when I tore my burning eyes from the screen, my fingers still moved of their own accord, pouring out art like a waterfall.

Heart pounding and desperate to make it stop, to give my hands a reprieve, I took my cast iron mallet with my non-dominant hand and slammed it on the back of my writing hand. I bit back a scream, but my hand refused to stop, so I hit it again and again, hearing bone crunch as shockwaves of agony spread up my arm. My fingers twitched like the legs of a half-crushed insect still trying to escape its fate. My knees buckled when they stopped moving, and I fell unconscious before my head struck the floor.

I woke in agony, centered around my hand but radiating out the rest of my body. My right hand was bloody, bruised, and swollen to almost twice its size, with two fingers jutted out at odd angles. The sun had long gone down, and the clock on the microwave read 3:23 a.m. I struggled to push myself up, but my left arm shook and collapsed underneath me, unable to take the strain. My phone, though, was within reach, and I managed to pull it to me and dial 911 before passing out again.

I woke to bright fluorescent lights and the smell of citrus antiseptic. I wasn't in pain anymore because of the IV drip inserted into my left wrist. A cast covered my right hand. I examined it distantly as if it belonged to someone else. Maybe it had before I had taken a mallet to it. My head was quiet for the first time since I met Leah. I tried to think of a story, anything to occupy myself while I laid there gathering my thoughts, but nothing came. It was almost a blessed relief.

Eventually, a nurse poked her head in and then, seeing that I was awake, got the doctor.

When he appeared in the doorway with his clipboard in hand, he asked, "Ms. Hodgson?"

126

"Yes?"

"We've completed our initial examinations, and, well, I have questions. When the EMTs found you, you were unconscious with what appeared to be a self-inflicted broken hand. I must ask, was it self-inflicted?"

I nodded, my throat dry and my face warm. I must look like a crazy person to him.

He arched an eyebrow. "Would you feel comfortable telling me what happened?"

I shook my head, struggling to think of a believable lie. "I'd prefer not to talk about it. It's pretty embarrassing."

"Is it related to your severe dehydration, sleep deprivation, and malnourishment?"

Unsure of what else to say, I gave a slight shrug. "Maybe? The past few days have been a blur."

He looked up from his clipboard, shutting the door behind him. "Ms. Hodgson, before I ask this, I want to let you know anything you say will not leave this room. Legally, I cannot report you to the police, nor am I interested in doing so. There is no shame in it, and anything you divulge is protected by doctor-patient confidentiality. Do you understand?" I nodded, and he continued. "Are you on any illicit or controlled substances such as amphetamines, psychedelics, or opioids?"

I hesitated. It was the easy answer and would explain my malnourishment, exceptional productivity, and weight loss. Leah was like a drug in a way, I supposed. Whatever she did to inspire me was addictive, and I chose a fix over food and water. Even now, I longed for her warm embrace and whispered comforts in my ear. But my love for her wasn't anything illegal (in this country at least) and wouldn't show up on blood or urine tests. So, I shook my head. "No, I've never done anything harder than pot, and that was in college."

He eyed me suspiciously but didn't press. "Do you or your family

127

have a history of mental illness?"

"Some depression on my dad's side, but I don't struggle with it. I did go through a breakup recently, and it left me in a weird place." I mean, I thought we were broken up. She left me without a word, abandoning me to whatever strange spell she'd cast.

And suddenly, I was furious. Leah did this, and then she left me. I tuned out the doctor as he discussed my treatment plan. Because of the thorough breaks in my hand and the extreme wear and tear, I might not ever regain full use of it. But all I could think about was what I might have done to drive her away. She hadn't given me any indication of dissatisfaction in our relationship.

At this point, I could no longer deny her otherworldly nature. It took breaking my own hand to realize how unnatural she was. I'd dated before, fallen in love before, found muses in my girlfriends before, but nothing compared to the intensity of my compulsive desire to create had I ever felt the way I had felt as I did around Leah. I needed to find her and get answers.

They discharged me from the hospital after two days. I returned home to gather wooden stakes, the cast iron mallet, a clove of garlic, and anything else I'd read would protect against supernatural beings. Leah and I needed to talk, and I knew just where to find her.

She sat at our usual picnic table, serenely staring up at the blue sky like she did the day we met. The summer cicadas buzzed a low drone while a breeze carrying the last vestiges of spring rustled through the trees. "I see you have rejected my gift."

"Who are you?" I demanded, ignoring the comment, and brandishing the mallet.

Languidly, she pulled her eyes away from the sky to meet mine. "I am called Leanan-Sidhe by most humans and Leah by the ones I have grown to like. I know you have questions, so ask, and I will do my best to answer."

"What did you do to me?"

Leah sighed, and I could see the deep well of sadness in her beautiful eyes, centuries' worth of grief seeping through the placid surface.

"Once every seven years, I am permitted to wander among the humans from one summer solstice to the next. I always fall in love with someone—an artist—and inspire greatness but at a price. When I'm with them, they waste away, neglecting themselves in favor of creating their art. When I leave, they're so shocked by the sudden silence after a cacophony of ideas that they inevitably suffer from an art block that most cannot overcome in their lifetimes. And so, their soul dies before the body. Most end up taking their own lives. When I saw you begin wasting away like the others, I knew I had to do something. So, I gave you a boon. Even after I'm gone, you'll never have to worry about suffering from a writer's or art block. I had hoped it was a loophole that would let you live and remain an artist."

"Leah, if I hadn't broken my hand, I would have died," I said, feeling dizzy with the revelation.

She looked at me uncomprehendingly, like a puppy that had been told no for the very first time. "I—I don't...."

I explained to her the events of yesterday and my realization that she wasn't human. "I couldn't stop, no matter how much I wanted to. It was awful." My hands shook with the memory of the ordeal, nausea welling up inside me. I clenched them into fists, letting my fear and pain turn into outrage. "And for what? I never asked for fame, fortune, or greatness. I never asked to waste away, compelled to create and create even as my body rebelled against me. I never wanted this. My art was for me and me alone until I met you, and I liked it that way. Why did you do this to me?"

By the end of my little speech, I'd shouted loud enough to disturb the birds in the trees and gain the attention of bystanders. Leah's eyes blazed with a fury that awoke the long-forgotten feeling of being prey to a much stronger hunter.

"You ungrateful child. I've had men fall upon their swords for the

129

chance to meet me, and women give up everything they'd ever known for even a scrap of the love I've felt for you and the inspiration you'd received. How dare you?"

I let out a bitter laugh as tears blurred my vision. "How dare me? How dare you presume that I wanted what you gave me?"

The blaze in her eyes became an inferno. She straightened her back, drawing herself to her full height, looking down at me like I was nothing more than an insect to be crushed beneath her thumb. I took an involuntary step back at the sight, and her lips curled into a wolfish smile.

"Very well. If you hate the greatness that I offered you, I can promise that no one will ever see your art again."

A cold shiver ran down my spine while the air around me crackled with a strange energy. Between one blink and the next, she was gone. I never saw her again.

That afternoon, I received an email from my publisher saying they couldn't open any of my novel's drafts. The documents kept appearing blank to them. Then, I got a call from the gallery informing me all my art had been stolen. The guests were reporting blank canvases on the walls in place of my paintings. Yet, I could still easily open my word documents, and the photos that the security guard sent of the missing paintings looked to me like all the paintings were in their proper place.

Suddenly, I understood. Leah, in her anger, laid a curse that no one could see my art except me. When I doodled on a napkin at a restaurant, no one saw it even after I pointed it out. When sent away, my writing would appear as blank word documents, and people suddenly found themselves partially deaf whenever I sang or hummed.

I know that no one is reading this. You physically cannot read it, but after my hand recovered, I returned to journaling. No one would believe me if I told them what truly happened, so it was a way to explore my feelings without the fear of everyone reading it.

My feelings about Leah now are conflicted. I loved her—or at least thought I was in love with her—and she became my muse. She offered friendship, romance, and wealth. I wouldn't have gotten as far as I did without her. She pushed me to become the great artist I was always meant to be. I loved her, even though I hated her for the way she upended my life.

To love the fae is to invite madness, but the truly insane part is, if she were to appear on my doorstep tomorrow, I'd take her back; consequences be damned.

AUTHOR BIO

Kay Hanifen was born on a Friday the 13th and once spent three months living in a haunted 14th-century castle. So, obviously, she had to get into horror writing. She's a certified monster-nerd and a former contributor to Screen Rant. Her short stories have appeared in the *Strangely Funny VII*, *Crunchy with Ketchup*, and *Midnight from Beyond the Stars* anthologies. When she isn't reading, writing, and taking in pop culture with the voraciousness of a vampire at a twenty-four-hour blood bank, you can find her on Twitter @TheUnicornComi1.

SEASONS END

BY C. MARRY HULTMAN

The house in which my aunt lived happened to be one of those storybook cottages. Like those you read about in old children's books, you know, like the imaginative retellings of stories by the Brothers Grimm. In those stories, the major characters read as poor and on the brink of starvation, but you wouldn't know it by looking at their home. Thatched roof, white brick walls, and tiny windows that look over pretty wildflower gardens, ample berry bushes, and a lazy crick flowing right behind it.

I always assumed my aunt, who left me the house when she was at the ripe old age of 98, lived a life as quaint as her home. However, deciding to settle there in the fall of 1982, I soon came to understand that, like the Grimm's fairy tales, the true story held more wonder and amazement than I could have imagined.

"I am thrilled the house will come to good use," Mary Olsen, the realtor, told me as we stood at the black wrought-iron gates viewing

133

my aunt's home.

"My mother always wanted it to remain in the family," I replied. "It used to belong to their parents."

"Yes, I saw that on the deed. Three generations of Spooner residents. That is impressive."

"My mom always said my great-grandfather built the cottage with his own two hands," I opened the gate and carried my bag up the well-manicured garden path. "My siblings and I never believed it."

"Will they be interested in the house as well?" Mrs. Olsen waddled up next to me, notepad in hand.

"No," I said, stopping and looking out over the wild garden comprised of berry bushes, fruit trees, and assorted flowers. "They passed a few years ago."

"I am sorry to hear that."

"Did you mow the lawn?" I asked, surprised at how well kept everything was. "I thought my aunt disappeared over a year ago."

"She did," Mrs. Olsen replied, looking at her orthopedic shoes. "The neighbor, Mr. Masefield, tended to the garden. It's something he'd done the last few years your aunt was alive."

The word, *alive*, grated down my spine. I remembered Aunt Annie as a vivacious woman always dressed in bright, colorful mismatched outfits. Every time we traveled to visit her, she would explode out the blue front door and dance down the path towards us.

It had always been the same ritual. Aunt Annie would sweep my little sister, Em, up into her arms and twirl around like a dervish while I looked sideways at my older brother, Chris, who rolled his eyes. He hated taking the eight-hour trip every summer. Chris was always acting like a typical teenager, but he had enjoyed skulking off

134

into the woods by himself, searching for adventure.

But now Aunt Annie was gone. Earlier in the year, the police stood on my porch and told me my aunt had gone missing. For how long she'd been missing, no one knew. One of the neighbors had noticed my aunt's lights no longer turning on at night, and they suspected she had wandered off one day and never found her way back. The police thought maybe she had fallen into the creek that ran into Yellow River, and she drowned. They dredged the waterways, but they never found her.

As I was the only one left in the family, I inherited the cottage.

"Do you intend to sell it, Miss Petersen?" Mrs. Olsen asked, handing me the keys.

"No, I'm going to keep it for now," I replied. "I sold my house in Racine. I felt that a change of scenery was necessary."

"Well, Washburn County is a magical place," Mrs. Olsen smiled. "Far away from the busy life of the city, and this cottage is even away from the beaten path. Only a few houses along this road."

She pointed to the gravel road that ran parallel to the main dirt road beyond the trees.

"I assume your furniture is coming later?" She continued to chatter as I opened the blue door and stepped inside.

"No, I sold it all as well," I said, breathing in the stale air and considering the furniture covered by white sheets.

"Well, your aunt left everything," she indicated the cottage at large. "All paid for as well."

From the inside, the cottage always felt larger than it appeared to be from the outside: three bedrooms, a library, kitchen, dining room, and a bathroom. Small for a family of six, which they had been

135

when my mother and aunt were young, but it was more than adequate for a single person.

The front door opened to the kitchen. We walked through, past the dining room on the right, and turned into the library on the opposite side.

"It's as I remember it," I said and looked at the walls lined with floor-to-ceiling walnut bookshelf. "Not an inch uncovered."

"She sure liked to read," Mrs. Olsen said and tapped the faded spine of a copy of Jürgen.

"She would read to us every night. Right here by the fireplace. We would drink warm cider and listen to her voice take us away to other worlds."

"I recall her doing it at the library as well. The kids loved her. Such a shame what happened to her."

I sighed and pulled the sheet off her favorite chair, a monster of comfort with soft velvet cushions. It sat next to a dark wood side table. I let my hand run across the soft back and looked at a sketch of the Eiffel Tower on the wall.

"Did you draw that?" Mrs. Olsen asked.

"I think I know better than making the Eiffel Tower gold," I smiled. "Even as a kid. No, I think Aunt Annie did it herself. She always said she was going to die in Paris."

"Die in Paris?"

"It was some queer obsession she had." I thought back to all those times she would burst through her bedroom door and scream those words. "She said it all the time. *One day, Tessa, I will die in Paris.* Never understood what she meant."

"She never got there," Mrs. Olsen sighed.

"I would like to think she did," I smiled and picked up a book from the side table. The book was hardcover in blue felt. A boy in a classic British school uniform embossed in gold on the cover. The title of the book read *Queen of Sunset Town*. I had never seen it before and turned it over, but it lacked a blurb.

"Well, I better be off then," Mrs. Olsen said. "I am sure you would like to settle in and wash off the road. My husband came in a few days ago and ran the water and made sure the toilet flushed."

"Thank you," I said, ignoring her.

She left, and I placed the book back on the table. Then removed the rest of the sheets in the library, and once they lay in a heap on the old oriental rug, I walked around the bookshelves and ran my fingers over the familiar spines: *The Lion, the Witch, and the Wardrobe, The Worm Ouroboros, The Midnight Folk*. Aunt Annie had read them all to us. I don't know how long I wandered the literary path when a sudden noise from the kitchen pulled me back to the present.

I waited a moment to be certain I'd heard something. Had Mrs. Olsen returned? A shuffling noise followed, and I grabbed a fire poker and moved towards the kitchen.

I dashed into the room only to find it empty—everything in its place except for the sheet covering the kitchen table and a chair. The fabric had moved to one side while one of the wooden chairs lay turned over. I raised the poker and glanced around, then I moved to the kitchen and discovered a door ajar. Someone had been in the house. Returning to the kitchen, I peered out of the solitary, round window over the sink. It faced the garden and the stream. Suddenly, I saw a boy, who appeared to be about eleven years of age, run down the path towards the woods. He wore a red school uniform and atop his head a felt cap. Blond locks danced around his ears as he darted through the gate.

I froze in amazement, not sure if I wanted to catch him or not. As if he could sense my hesitation, he halted near the stone wall and turned to me. He gave me an impish smile and winked, and then he waved for me to come out. My eyes narrowed as I considered it, then made my move.

By the time I had burst through the door, the kid had vanished. I walked towards the spot I had last seen him and thought about it all. His outfit had looked almost archaic. He'd worn preparatory uniform, red jacket, striped tie, and gray slacks. As far as I was aware, there were no private schools in Spooner or Washburn County.

Then I heard it. The soft lilting tones of a solitary fiddle carried on the wind. I felt mesmerized by it and, without realizing it, walked towards the origins. I didn't need to venture far from the house because a young man sat on some water slick rocks in the middle of the creek. Pale and slender with hair down to his shoulders, he played his fiddle in a way I had never before heard.

"Hey," I shouted at the youth.

He ceased, tilted his head, and looked at me.

"Sorry for interrupting," I continued, startled at the fact that he was naked. "Did you see a young kid come through here? In a red jacket?"

The young man placed the fiddle and bow down on the rocks and turned his body towards me. I took a step back and felt my face flush at the brazen nakedness of the hairless youth.

138

"Pardon me?" he said in a voice as flowery as the instrument he played.

"Did you see a little kid run past?"

"I see many things?" The man smiled, and his eyes twinkled like the sun reflecting in a clear mountain stream.

"Did you see that?" I grew irritated.

"I did," he replied and picked up the fiddle again.

"Where did he go?"

"He vanished. He does that," he placed the bow on the strings.

"Did he go off into the woods?"

"I told you. The boy vanished. He is not here anymore. You decide if you wish to chase him or not."

"Come on," I shouted. "Just let me know where the boy went so that I can ask him why he was at my house."

"Kai is nowhere and everywhere," the man replied and played. "You will find him, but the question is if you want to catch him."

As the sun set, I spent the rest of the evening restoring the cottage to its former glory, or at least the way I remembered it, even though I was still seething from my conversation with the naked man in the stream. I felt somewhat ashamed of how irritated he made me, but anger came quicker and quicker in recent years.

The truth was, I needed to get away from the city, away from my past, but to what I still didn't know. My life had become an endless downward spiral. My parents and siblings had passed, and suddenly I had no sense of direction or purpose. I had nothing other than a string of failed relationships, dead-end jobs, and an education with which I could do nothing. More than not, I found myself curled up in a fetal position, weeping without control.

When I received the letter informing me I'd inherited my aunt's cottage, I didn't hesitate. She always seemed like she'd had it together. Even if she was eccentric, perhaps even on the verge of crazy, she never had to chase the specter of joy. No, she found real happiness right here in her family home. On the other hand, my mother had died miserable and filled with regret, and regretfully, I saw myself following in my mother's footsteps.

Once I had a fire lit and everything cleaned up, I was ready to settle down with a glass of red wine. As I relaxed in Aunt Annie's favorite chair, I once again picked up the felt-covered book and looked at the cover. I ran my fingers over the image of the uniformed child embossed on the surface. It looked like the boy the naked violinist had called Kai. I possibly would have chalked the encounter up to a trick of the mind, but if the boy in the garden weren't real, then the violinist wouldn't have known about him.

I decided not to dwell on it and instead picked up a larger book on the side table. Like an enormous square, this book resembled a scrapbook. Hoping to find some old family photos, I opened it only to be startled to find newspaper clippings instead.

The clippings were yellowed and brittle, and I was careful not to tear them. They all had one common theme: the disappearance of various family members. My mother never told me what had happened to my grandparents. I had just assumed they had died before my birth, but according to an article, they had vanished one day. Aunt Annie had come home to find them gone. There were margins near older clippings that all told the same story. Generations of my family had mysteriously gone missing. The last page had a scrap of paper torn from a notebook, and it contained a historical list of the cottage's residents—each with a question mark next to it. The page even had the names of my mother and siblings jotted down between the college-ruled lines. However, instead of questions marks after each name, there were crosses.

I looked up and saw the boy in the uniform silhouetted in the moonlight. He stood in the doorway, observing me. I rose, and he vanished towards the exit. I followed, but by the time I reached the blue door, he had disappeared again. The door swung on its hinges behind him.

I shuffled back to the library only to find the blue book glowing with an eerie greenish glow—a low hum, like a melody playing in an adjacent room, emitted from it. Carefully I moved closer to it, my fingers trembling as they reached out.

The hum transformed into a tune; I could hear both laughter and joyful music played on an accordion. It grew in intensity until the light became blinding. I felt drawn to it in the same way the violin music had lured me previously. The book controlled me, tugging at my body to come closer. I felt an urge to obey, but I was not willing to submit. I swatted the book away from the table, sent it across the room, and left it on the floor. The melody stopped, and the light died, leaving me only with the glow from the dying fire.

"Welcome to the neighborhood," a voice said to me the following morning when I ventured outside. "Such as it is."

Groggily, I turned to find a tall gentleman leaning on the stone fence. He had a big bushy black beard, and he wore a beret and green overalls. He smiled at me with a pipe in his mouth and touched his nose with his index finger.

"Excuse me?" I asked. "Who are you?"

The man burst into a deep, infectious laugh. "My name is Masefield," he said. "I've been caring for the house since your aunt disappeared."

"Well, thank you," I said. "You live next door, right?"

"In a way," he pointed to somewhere in the distance. "I live a couple of miles up the road."

"Did you know my aunt well?"

"I conversed with her occasionally. We exchanged pleasantries. Nothing more than that."

"Do you know anything about her disappearance?"

"Not a clue," Masefield took a puff on his pipe. "She had periods of melancholy, and during the weeks before she vanished, she felt very low. That is all I can say. She was an exceptional woman, though."

"Yes," I replied and made to turn. "Do you know of a little kid in a uniform that runs around here?"

"Don't worry about him." Masefield winked at me. "He only wants you to chase him."

"What do you mean?"

"You decide if that is what you want to do," he rose from the wall. "Stay safe, Miss Peterson. Stay safe."

He walked away down the trail towards the main road, and no wiser than before, I returned to the house.

Then, in the kitchen window, I saw the little toe-headed boy looking at me. I saw him laugh then vanish. I sprinted towards the house and ran into the kitchen. As expected, he was gone. Then I heard the melodic hum from the previous night, and I stepped into the library.

The blue book lay open on the center of the floor, not where I had flung it. The hum had turned into a perfect melody with proper instruments again. I could make out an accordion, a violin, and maybe a clarinet. The music pulled me in with more force than before; I felt helpless in fighting it. My legs moved beyond my control, and once I stood beside the book, it hovered up towards me. My eyes hurt from the golden glow as the pages drew closer to my face. The music, almost deafening now, enveloped me, and the warmth of a summer breeze welcomed me in. Then it felt as if I disintegrated into millions of atoms as I was sucked into oblivion.

I came to on a large hill. The grass was so soft and lush it felt reminiscent of the softest duvet cover. The grass was only slightly damp with early morning dew, yet warm enough that it felt divine on my skin.

I sat up and gazed at the world stretched out below. Before me, vast fields of sunflowers spread as far as the eye could see. In the distance, I saw what appeared to be a single path leading into a village. Rising beyond the town stood the Eiffel Tower, but golden, sparkling in the bright sunlight. It was beautiful in the clear blue sky. I heard something move behind me, and I looked around and saw large pages floating in the air. Cream-colored pages from a book were hanging in the air. As they moved, I could see writing in a language I did not recognize, along with illustrations of my aunt's cottage.

143

A strange sensation of calm came over me. I knew I should have felt fear in this strange world, but I was at ease. There was no immediate need to return home, which I assumed was through the pages. Instead, I decided to investigate where the path lead.

Turning around, I found the boy, Kai, standing there. He winked at me and then ran away, running down the path with his hands holding his cap in place. This time I felt no anger. I laughed and chased after him. I kept laughing because it seemed like I floated on air. I'd never been an athletic person, but surprisingly, I didn't feel sweaty or out of breath at the task. The music from earlier returned. First, low and in the distance, then louder and with greater intensity.

We followed the winding path, past fields of golden wheat and rapeseed. Moss-covered stone fences lined the way, and soon cows and sheep took the place of plants.

Soon we were at the outskirts of the village, where rows upon rows of white cottages stood with thatched roofs. A cobbled stone street lead down the center. The boy slowed down, turned around, and beckoned me to follow. I obeyed and walked behind him as he skipped down the street. As if caught in some wondrous dream, I looked at the idyllic houses and saw other people for the first time.

Young and old, they were all dressed in clothes from the turn of the century. Some were hanging wet clothes on a line, while others were feeding chickens in their yards. Occasionally, the homes gave away to businesses. The smell of fresh bread from a bakery wafted past me. A man at a stand sold fresh produce, and a butcher stood in a bloody apron, cutting up a hog.

We reached a square, and now the golden structure towered over us. The Eiffel Tower stretched towards the heavens like the

144

hands of sinners reaching for salvation. A fountain stood in the middle of the square, water dancing rhythmically in time with the joyous music played by the street performers sitting around it. It was the same melody again. A small café had set up tables beside the fountain, and a skinny server with a pointy nose and a pencil-thin mustache served various guests conversing with one another.

"Tessa," came a familiar voice from the tables.

Rising from her seat, dressed in a blue and yellow summer dress, was Aunt Annie. Her long, dark hair cascading over her shoulders as she walked towards me with arms outstretched.

"Aunt Annie," I said, overcome with surprise and emotion.

"You made it," she wrapped me in a warm embrace, and I broke down.

The emotions of the past year bubbled up to the surface, and I couldn't hold them in. I cried into the soft fabric of the shawl that covered her shoulders.

"There, there, Tess," Annie said and caressed my head. "I know. You are here now."

She peeled me off and looked at me with concern in her eyes. She wiped a tear from my cheek and smiled. "Come, have a café au lait at my table and let me look at you."

"I have so many questions," I said as the server placed my café au lait before me.

"I'm sure you do," Annie replied and patted me on the hand. "It is wonderful to see you again. It has been an age."

"What is this place, and how are you here? How am I here?" I looked around at the busy square.

"One thing at a time, dear," she laughed. "I understand that this amazes you. It did the same to me when I met my parents again."

"Grandma and Grandpa are here too?" I asked and looked around.

"Not here, no. They are in their own place."

"Their *own* place? Do you mean they walked through another book?"

She laughed again. "It doesn't quite work that way. The book is only the portal. The people it lures decide the world it creates for them. Once the owner passes into the pages, the book has fulfilled its duty, and it will fade away until another person discovers it."

"I still don't get it. Where did it come from?"

"That is a question for the ages," Aunt Annie took a sip of her coffee. "Every single owner of the cottage has tried to figure it out. No one knows the origins. Some ancient magic from eons past. What I have found is that it might not have always been a book."

"What was it then?"

"Standing stones, a wardrobe, or a door in a tree. Who knows? For as long as it's been in our family, it's been a book."

"And you walked into it?" I doubted my faculties at this point.

"When I felt ready to leave our world, yes, I did. I built this place over time. My wants and needs created it. This is a representation of my vision of a perfect world. It is not an exact copy of what I'd dreamed, but it's close enough."

"The French countryside? With the Eiffel Tower."

"It is how I imagined a rural Paris from long ago. Not quite accurate, but I've never been there."

"*One day, I will die in Paris,*" I whispered.

146

"That's right, you remember! It is enough to place the Eiffel Tower anywhere, and suddenly, it becomes Paris," she furrowed her brows. "Maybe I should have thought of Notre Dame or the Arc de Triomphe, but hey, this place is lovely."

"What about all the people that live here? Who are they?" I said, nodding my head in the direction of the server.

"Memories of people I have met over the years," Annie replied. "Those who, for some reason, left their mark on me. They aren't real, but they are pleasant to talk with."

"Are you dead?" I asked in disbelief.

"In some kind of limbo, perhaps," she replied. "This book is fading now that you have settled in the house. My story is ending, and yours is about to take shape."

"So, you're dying?"

"That is probably more correct. No one ever tells us anything here."

"If this is *your* perfect place," I began as we walked towards the tower. "Why am I here?"

"You," Annie's smile turned into a frown.

"I don't follow."

"Just like it was with me years ago, you asked the questions. *What do I want to do with my life? Where am I headed? Is there no one out there to take pity on me?* It is a tough time, believe me, I know. You stare into the black abyss—the void of despair and self-doubt. You went through severe trauma when your mother died and then your siblings. I am sorry that I couldn't be there for you, but that need brought you here today."

147

"To learn about this world?"

"To learn how to create your own. To stop chasing someone else's dream and start realizing what you want. I had to go through it. My parents as well, and as far as I know, everyone in our family."

"What about that little blond kid," I asked. "The one in the uniform?"

"Kai?" We halted right under the massive golden structure. Annie looked up at it and smiled. "He is a manifestation born somewhere between reality and imagination. He needs you to chase him; he thrives on your need to chase him. Think of him as your childhood, innocence lost, whatever obsession you are trying to catch. The best days of your life, what have you."

"And what about the naked guy in the creek?" I leaned against one of the massive legs and felt the cold steel through my clothes.

"Näcken? He's been around for years. He came with the first Swedish settlers to Spooner. Formed by the same magic as the book, and maybe Masefield."

"Him too?"

"I don't know what he is, to be honest. Näcken is an old world fae, but Masefield is something else." Aunt Annie looked at the sun in the sky. "We need to move on before this day has passed."

She began walking and gestured for me to join her. We ventured up a small hill, and once we reached the top of it, Annie pointed to a cavern dug into the side of an opposite hill.

"For now, this is your destiny." She wore a somber look.

"What now?" I asked.

"To find your truth, you must venture into that cave over there. Pass through it is all. I'll be waiting here." She placed her hand

148

on my back and pushed me down the slope and towards the cave.

The warmth and brightness of the perpetual summer's day vanished as I stepped into the cave. A chill ran up my spine as I walked further down. Aunt Annie had given me a flashlight, and I shone it on the stone walls surrounding me. The ceiling stood only a foot or so above, and the large stalactites hanging from overhead threatened to hit my head. Suddenly Kai stood before me. His blond hair shone in the lamplight. He chuckled and then turned to walk.

Following close behind, I made sure not to lose sight of him. I quickened my step to match his but lost sight of him as he rounded a corner. Hot on his heels, I did the same, but around the corner, I met a mirror unexpectedly. My reflection looked back at me, but it wore a school uniform like Kai instead of my clothes.

I turned, only to be met by another mirror. This time my reflection wore the old, stained pajamas I had worn for nearly three months during the worst part of my downward spiral. I tried another direction, but again there was another mirror and another doppelganger. This time my reflection had the gray pallor of the dead, with hollow cheeks and sunken eyes. The fourth mirrored wall showed a thin figure, pale as the third, but dark damp hair hid its face. I couldn't find an exit; I was trapped in a maze of my reflection.

I backed away, right into a cold mirror with a horrid image of myself. I moved to the middle of the cube I now found to be my prison. I tried to scream, but no sound escaped. I curled into a ball as the horrid reflection came closer. My uniformed double kneeled and looked at me.

"You must decide, here and now," she said with a small, hollow voice. "Which future do you choose?" It rose again. "Look

149

around. We are all the possibilities, one worse than the next. Except for me, of course. I am what you always wanted. Your deepest desire. Choose me, and I will lead you in an eternal, merry dance."

I rocked back and forth, hugging my knees. I couldn't wrap my mind around the choice, the reflections, or their demands. What could bring me joy? Then I realized that this was the point of no return.

Come on down and meet your maker
Come on down and make the stand

The words echoed in my head, and I rose with the flashlight in my hand. The uniformed reflection smiled at me and held its hands up in a defensive position. The deafening sound of glass breaking danced between the walls, and splintered glass rained on me.

"It is done then?" Aunt Annie smiled as I walked out of the cave.

"I broke your flashlight," I replied and handed it to her.

"I'll recover," she looked up into the sky again. "It's time."

I felt a single tear form and roll down my face as I grabbed her hand.

"Please come with me. I need you." I pleaded.

"Sorry Tess, I can't," she whispered and wiped my cheek dry with a thumb. "Remember what I always told you when you were younger."

"That you were going to die in Paris," I looked at the shiny Eiffel Tower glistening in the setting sun. "But this isn't it."

"It is my vision of Paris," she moved my head to look at her

150

again. "I don't belong in your world anymore. I can't be there to hold your hand. It's time for you to stand on your own two feet. You must meet your challenges head-on and be your own person."

"But I don't know how," I replied.

"Yes, you do," Annie said. "It can be hard to find, but deep down, there is an answer." She placed her other hand over my heart.

"I just need..."

"You have everything you need," she interrupted. "Step through those pages, and you will be back in the cottage in Spooner. Then place the book back on the shelf, and the door to this world will close forever."

"What if I want to visit again?"

"That can never happen. Once you close the book, the story ends. You must find your own portal, the one that leads you to the world you create. A place you belong." She kissed me on the cheek and released me. "Now go. This is where we part ways."

In tears, I stepped away from her. I didn't want to leave—every fabric of my being urged me to stay. I turned to the enormous book. Its pages moved in the slight breeze. I looked back for a moment, but the world had already begun disintegrating. The scene was out of focus. The only object still clearly visible was the golden tower growing ever distant.

"It's getting close to seasons end," Aunt Annie smiled.

The following morning, I stood at the window in my kitchen. With a fresh cup of coffee in my hands, I watched the sun steadily climb over the treetops. A fine mist danced through the trunks playing with the dew on the green grass. I contemplated the events of the previous day

151

and what I had learned. After exiting my aunt's world through the book, I woke up on the floor of the library. At first, I was confused, but I pieced it together after a few glasses of wine.

The portal seemed forever closed now. The book was only blank pages, and the figure on the blue cover was no more than an outline. I left the book open on the side table, hoping the golden tower would again appear, knowing that if it didn't, Aunt Annie would be gone forever.

As the world outside my window woke from slumber, my gaze followed the creek until it landed on the slender youth, sitting naked on the grassy shore with his feet in the stream. He looked back, winked, and smiled at me. The fiddle was resting next to him. So at least Näcken would always be part of my world. He nodded towards the dirt road, and my heart sank as the figure of Kai appeared at the stone wall. His red school uniform was covered in dust, and his knees were slathered with mud. He smiled at me and doffed his cap, letting his shock of golden curls glisten like the Eiffel tower in the morning sun.

He gave me a curious smile. The same one he had flashed me the first night I chased him. Then he darted off into the woods, down the path along the creek. Näcken laughed as he watched Kai stop at the edge of the wood, turning back towards the cottage. Kai beckoned me to chase him once again.

I looked down at the cup in my hand, the dark liquid rippling, reminiscent of the black abyss of my life. I looked back at Kai, who waited, arms crossed. He looked different somehow, more grown, brow furrowed in annoyance at my tardiness.

I placed my cup in the kitchen sink, considering what the

future may hold. Maybe the time for aimlessly chasing the unknown was over.

I walked back into the library. The pages of Aunt Annie's book were crisp and white now. Picking it up, I sat down in the chair and thought about what I would want to write in my own book and how my perfect world would appear. I imagined becoming the person I truly wanted to be in a place filled with my dreams and desires and compiled of all the places I longed to visit.

AUTHOR BIO

C. Marry Hultman is a teacher, writer and sometimes podcaster who is equal parts Swede and Wisconsinite. He lives with his wife and two daughters and runs W.A.R.G -The Guild podcast dedicated to interviewing authors about their creative process. In addition to that, he runs the website Wisconsin Noir - Cosmic Horror set in the Dairy State where he collects short fiction and general thoughts.

THE SHARD

WILLIAM TUDOR

Saturday 13ʰ August 1898, London

From a very early age Simon Westcott, a progeny of an affluent middle-class family in his twenty-third year, had begun to suffer a relentless and gnawing dissatisfaction with the domain of physical reality; the everyday world of flesh and blood and what he perceived to be the trivial and mundane concerns of his peers. This sense of unease had only increased with age, eventually leading him to study mysticism, alchemy, and the occult sciences. For Simon, the wants and desires of ordinary men were not enough; he was driven by something deeper, a need to penetrate the veils of the physical world, to know the hidden reality that is usually barred from the senses of men.

On that particular morning, Simon had awoken early and was busy tidying the large two-bedroom second-floor apartment he called home in the fashionable area of Grosvenor Square, London. When everything was in order, Simon surveyed the large living room area with its heavy oak furniture, oxblood chesterfield sofas, and floor-to-ceiling windows that overlooked the opulent Mayfair gardens beyond. He then turned his attention to the equally large master bedroom dedicated exclusively to his occult practices.

Everything in this room was meticulously arranged. Towering oak bookcases lined each sidewall, adorned with heavy volumes of occult literature and esoteric artifacts, from Arabic daggers to ornate chalices and jars filled with various herbs and incenses. A small cabinet next to the large ornate open fireplace contained various alchemical paraphernalia, including stacks of raw minerals and jars containing mercury and sulphuric acid obtained through Simon's carefully cultivated connections at the local University. A large table draped in black silk at the far end of the room served as an altar. It contained two large and ornate brass candlesticks positioned on either side of an empty wooden stand, similar to an artist's tabletop easel, clearly intended to hold the focal point to an occult ceremony.

Before closing the heavy crimson blackout drapes, Simon proudly surveyed space before him. He then carefully exited the room as though any sudden movement could disturb the dark stillness that perpetually lingered and permeated the area.

Taking his tweed jacket from the nearby stand and placing it over one arm, he paused to regard himself in the full-length mirror in the hallway next to the main door to his apartment. Simon was pleased by what he saw: a tall and strongly built man who liked to dress well and looked after himself. His face was symmetrical and handsome, with pale grey eyes and high cheekbones framed by a shock of wavy blonde hair that billowed from his crown. It was at striking variance to the current trend for neat and slicked styles and served as an ongoing bone of contention with his conservative father, for whom he worked in the family banking and finance firm.

In truth, Simon had always seen himself as something of a rebel, an *enfant terrible* amongst the more conventional individuals within his wealthy family and circles of acquaintance. He had always been popular with girls too, even though he may not have always realized it, being, as he often was, so distracted by more otherworldly pursuits. Besides, the only person Simon had any real time for was Lucy, his girlfriend of two years. She was someone for whom Simon cared most deeply and even hoped to marry one day, despite her coming from a wealthier family and possessing a father who made no secret of his disapproval of their relationship.

That morning Simon had an appointment with Oscar Jones, the proprietor of the *Lux Hermetica* occult book and supply shop nestled in the back streets of bohemian London. Oscar had finally been able to procure a particularly rare ceremonial artifact that Simon had sought for some time, a ritual item used by the notorious 17th-century witch, Aida Merryck. It was a large shard of obsidian that Merryck used for seership rituals that she called the 'mirror of Andras.' It was dedicated to a demon of the same name. This demon frequently appeared in the manuscripts of medieval thaumaturgy that Simon had studied fastidiously in the tiny back rooms of the British Museum library, often until the early hours of the morning.

According to Merryck's documented confessions shortly before her brutal execution at the hands of inquisitors in 17th century Derbyshire, the mirror is a gateway between dimensions. It is a means to communicate with otherworldly beings and can bestow great power upon the occultist bold to call upon the forces within it.

Simon opened the front door to his apartment. He slipped outside, heading down through the luxurious alabaster marble staircase with its flawless sage green walls and luscious Boston ferns that sprawled in great tendrils above from hanging baskets that were placed at even intervals throughout the communal area. He eagerly pushed out through the building's main entrance to find the busy streets of this trendy part of middle-class London awash with activity. Commuters hurried to work, and the sound of hooves clashed on cobbles as horses pulled carriages filled with affluent families. He even could hear the sound of the occasional motorcar, which his father assured him was the next big investment opportunity.

As anxious as Simon was to get to the *Lux Hermetica*, he was possessed by a strong sense of vitality, a sudden awareness that he was about to embark upon something huge, something life changing. The *Lux* was a mere fifteen-minute walk away and tucked discreetly down a small alleyway that snaked away from the main high street. It was so unassuming that most of the people that passed it probably didn't even realize that it housed any shops at all. However, the *Lux Hermetica* was well known to the occultists and spiritualists of bohemian London.

Upon arrival, Simon paused briefly at the doorstep of the *Lux* to savor the moment before entering the little shop, and, when he did so, he was immediately greeted by the sights and smells he had come to know so well. His nostrils were filled with the smell of aromatic herbal incense, rich in sandalwood, jasmine, and patchouli. Along the perimeter walls were large ornate bookcases packed with books on every conceivable area of occultism and spirituality, all clearly labeled. Mythology, Qabalah, Buddhism, and spiritual philosophy lined the right-hand side of the shop's floor-length. The left wall housed books on witchcraft, magick, and runes. The center of the store's floor housed many display tables and cabinets. Various items were carefully arranged: ritual tools, statues of various gods and demons in varying sizes, and crystals and rare stones. A large Ashford black marble statue of the Egyptian cat goddess Bastet, the goddess of protection, sat prominently. At its base, a card bearing the words 'not for sale' had been carefully placed. Usually, Simon would spend considerable time examining each and every item, always looking for something to add to his collection. However, that day more pressing concerns drove him.

Walking up to the counter at the far end of the store, he saw Oscar Jones stooped over a stack of books that he appeared to be cataloging, likely new acquisitions for his store. Oscar is a lean and muscular gentleman in his early thirties. He had a freshly shaved head and a neatly trimmed

Machiavellian beard that was jet black and nicely complemented his olive skin. He was always dressed in a black collared shirt that he wore casually with the sleeves rolled up to the elbow, paired with matching black trousers and shoes.

Simon cautiously approached the counter, "Good morning, Oscar," he said in a gentle tone, as though reluctant to disturb a man so clearly engrossed in his work.

"Hello Simon, just give me a moment, would you?" Simon obliged and pretended to peruse a stack of journals that lay on a high table to his left, a few he recognized pertaining to some of the occult orders and fraternities that operated in and around London.

"Sorry about that," interrupted Oscar, "it has been quite a hectic month for both sales and acquisitions. Speaking of which, I have your procurement right here!" Oscar dipped into the small stock room that led from a narrow doorway behind the counter and quickly reappeared with a large flat bundle bound in a thick and aged canvas-type material. Placing it upon the worn countertop, Oscar paused to regard Simon.

"Now, you do understand precisely what you are dealing with here, don't you? This isn't a superficial curiosity to serve the vanity of an amateur. It is a precious antique and an occult piece of art. It is also a powerful ceremonial tool that could be very dangerous in the wrong hands. The seller is an Italian collector who wishes to remain anonymous."

"Do you happen to know how he acquired it?"

"No, *she* wouldn't tell me, but she did indicate that the mirror has been passed around various occult collectors throughout Europe for several generations now."

Oscar began to remove the artifact's bindings, continuing to talk as he did so. "I trust you are aware of the horror stories that surround the actual ritual use of this mirror? People have been driven mad, committed suicide, or homicide. The *lucky ones* have merely been haunted by

159

horrifying apparitions. I understand that those who have owned it in recent generations have only had it for display purposes. The previous owner claimed that she encountered an unusual phenomenon rather soon after acquiring it, so kept it bound in silk to act as a protective psychic barrier and stored it away out of harm's reach."

"So why sell now? Surely an item this valuable could have been sold for a high price at any time?"

"I asked her the same question. She told me she had wanted to keep it safely hidden and out of the wrong hands and that she is only selling now as she is with child."

"Ah!" The reason for the sale was suddenly abundantly clear.

"I mean it, Simon, this is not a joke. I didn't even want to handle it myself and never would have done so had it not been for my generous finder's fee. Speaking of which, do you have what we agreed?"

"I do indeed!" Simon enthused, pulling out a thick envelope of banknotes and placing it down on the counter.

Oscar picked up the envelope and peered inside, then, with a small, satisfied grunt of approval, tucked it under the counter without counting the cash. Oscar then returned his attention to the bundle once more, removing the last of the outer packing to reveal a layer of black silk tied with a red cord. His cautious hands slowly worked the artifact free from its final layer.

"And there it is!" said Oscar with a slight gasp, "the mirror of Andras! The actual mirror used by the witch Aida Merryck to communicate with demonic beings."

Oscar carefully handed the object to Simon and continued, "as you are no doubt aware, the few disciples of hers that evaded capture ransacked and looted her little cottage for various items that they thought would give them great power—which they *did* if the stories are to be believed. However, of all the artifacts that survived, this one possesses one of the worst reputations."

Simon held the mirror in hands that shook slightly; a shiver of

160

excitement ran up his spine. The mirror was cold and heavy. Simon was surprised by the unusual shape of the shard; it was like an elongated rectangle of sorts, narrower at the top then gradually widening towards the bottom; a raw slab of obsidian that was devoid of any sort of ornamentation or craftsmanship. The front side was completely clear of marks and looked highly polished. The reverse side had a large symbol etched into it; a symbol Simon recognized from the texts he had studied as the demon Andras' sigil. This side was also a little blemished and stained, no doubt due to being consecrated with blood and sexual fluids, as was Merrick's usual practice, according to her confessions.

"Fascinating!" said Simon, feeling a little breathless from adrenaline, the pace of his heart quickening to an uncomfortable pace.

"As you are no doubt aware," Oscar continued, "Merryck made pacts with many demonic beings: Lilith, Belial, and Astaroth are some of the more well-known ones, but she also made pacts with many of the more obscure demonic beings such as Vassago, Nesbiros and, of course, Andras. She was obsessed with dominion over the physical world and, if her confessions are to be believed, she was also a collector of souls."

Simon raised his eyebrows and tilted his head in subtle inquiry.

"Apparently," Oscar said, "the victims of her curses who fell slain became her puppets in the afterlife. Tools she could utilize to haunt and terrify the living. There has honestly never been an occultist as notorious or as genuinely dangerous as her. So please, *be careful*." Oscar paused for a moment and regarded Simon cautiously, as though what he was about to say next needed to be said with sensitivity and care.

"Are you sure about this, Simon? You know, it's not too late to back out of the deal, and I am more than happy to make some excuse or other to the seller. Besides, I know several members of the Mendesian brotherhood who would be more than keen to take this mirror off my hands today. It honestly wouldn't be any bother, and I don't want you to feel that you are now compelled in some way to see the deal through."

Simon briefly considered Oscar's words. The Mendesian Brotherhood was a Satanic Sect that held ceremonies in the attics of bohemian London's brothels and former dockland opium dens. Simon was irritated that Oscar had such little faith in him as an occultist and resented the implication that he was getting out of his depth. Besides, an artifact such as this was far too precious to be allowed into the hands of some juvenile sect of *poseurs* that, in Simon's mind, liked to dress up and play at black magic—a glorified gentleman's club of wealthy degenerates. Simon's resolve remained unshaken.

"Thank you very much, Oscar, but I feel that I am the best person to possess this mirror. I am, however, extremely grateful to you for obtaining this for me. You cannot even begin to imagine what this means."

With that, Simon said his goodbyes and hastily headed for home.

Upon returning to his building, Simon was greeted by Colin Reed, the portly concierge with black curly hair that looked after the building's residents. "Good morning, Mr. Westcott," he said as he greeted Simon warmly.

"Good morning, Mr. Reed."

"You have a letter waiting for you," continued Reed with well-practiced politeness, handing Simon a small envelope.

"Ah! Much obliged." Simon could see immediately from the delicate ornate handwriting that it was from Lucy. Simon leaned in against a marble pillar, his back turned towards the main foyer and Mr. Reed. With the bundle still secured under one arm, he quickly opened the letter to read it.

Dear Simon,
My driver and I will pick you up tonight around eleven P.M.
Wear something nice!
I want you to start making a good impression on Daddy!

162

Yours,

Lucy

"Damn!" Simon hissed under his breath, "The blasted dinner party!"

In the excitement, he had forgotten that he had long agreed to attend a gathering at Lucy's parents. However, as Lucy wouldn't be picking him up until late evening, he would still have plenty of time to complete his ritual and be ready for her arrival. It was inconvenient for sure but workable. With a perplexed sigh, Simon pushed up the stairway to his apartment to prepare for his work.

After entering the apartment, his first action was to go to his ceremony room and place the mirror upon the stand that stood upon his altar. He then returned to his living room and poured himself a generous scotch into a fine crystal cut tumbler, and reclined in his favorite chair, relishing the welcoming sound of creaking oak and leather as he relaxed into its plush dimensions.

Finally, he thought to himself triumphantly, taking in a mouthful of scotch, its warmth filling the pit of his stomach, immediately relaxing his body and mind. *Today, my work will finally be complete. If I can harness the power of the mirror of Andras, I will be unstoppable in all aspects of life. I can know for sure what investments to make, and I'll become rich! Even wealthier than my father! Or Lucy's, for that matter! Wouldn't that turn the tables somewhat! I can finally break free from the restrictions of work and become fully independent. I can dedicate my life to the powers of darkness.*

With a sense of excitement stirring in the pit of his stomach, Simon drained the whiskey and set the tumbler down on the table, then began to prepare for his ritual.

Simon had never really gone for the 'black robes and pentagram medallion' style ritual attire. In truth, he found it all a bit clichéd, not to mention more than a little *kitsch*. Instead, he preferred finely tailored suits meticulously crafted by the exclusive London tailors that he and his family had used for generations.

The particular piece he planned to wear this evening was a dark brown tweed suit with a mustard-colored waistcoat, beige silk shirt, and a dark yellow silk bow tie. Expensive but worth it for the ritual to feel right. After all, when summoning demons from the outer void, a person must look their best.

Before entering the ceremony room, he paused to regard himself in the long hallway mirror as though the events that were about to unfold would change him permanently. He wanted to take stock of himself beforehand as though taking one last look at an infected limb before it was permanently amputated.

Entering the temple room, Simon began by lighting the candles placed in ornate candelabras positioned around the room to give an even distribution of light. He also lit the large open fireplace to add further light and warmth to the room, which was always unnaturally cold despite the time of year. He then went to the altar and, reaching underneath, pulled out his ritual tools which included a bell, a dagger, an ornate wand, and a wooden disk containing a carved pentagram which he positioned upon the altar top before the mirror.

Lastly, he pulled out the most important item of all, the brown leather ledger in which he had transcribed his rituals.

Simon began to meditate until he achieved a state of single-pointed focus, and his breathing slowed down to a deep and steady rhythm. When he felt ready, Simon opened his eyes. He took up the ritual text and his wand, with which he began to perform incantations with force and vigor, allowing the words to penetrate the dimensions beyond his physical and worldly senses. Throughout all of this, he noticed that *something* was

164

happening, something tangible. It was as though the areas of the room illuminated by the candlelight and fireplace, which now roared violently, had crystallized, and become more vivid. Conversely, the parts of the room cast in shadow were growing darker with a blackness that stirred and swelled with every word he spoke, like a boiling pot of heaving black tar.

With the energy in the room having reached the necessary intensity, Simon prepared to establish communication with the demon Andras through the mirror and positioned himself before the altar. He performed a prepared evocation aimed at the demon and then began to chant the ceremonial formula to open the gates of Hell.

Zazas, Zazas, Nasatanada Zazas

As he chanted, he stared intensely into the blackened depths of the mirror, falling ever deeper and deeper into a trance. It wasn't long before he lost awareness of everything except the seething dark energy surrounding him.

Time, matter, and form became meaningless as Simon's consciousness became fused with the mirror, the portal to the outer voids for which he had lusted for so long. In the depths of the abyss before him, he began to see something, an undulating mass writhing in the distance, nebulous and unformed yet starting to grow and take shape.

Simon felt his heart seize with trepidation as he beheld the vision before him take on a humanoid appearance. It was growing bigger too, or was it getting closer?

Fear began to take hold of Simon. He had prepared for this day for so long, had yearned for it constantly, but what was transpiring before him was disconcertingly real. All Simon could do was focus upon his breathing to steady himself.

The figure was becoming more vivid. Simon could now see a human-like figure garbed in black robes that billowed as though disturbed by an underwater current. Simon's brow creased; something wasn't right.

165

The figure manifesting before him didn't conform to the descriptions of the demon Andras, who was described as a raven-headed man carrying a sword and riding upon the back of a large black wolf. Rather, the figure before him was a tall, slender woman with long raven black hair and skin the color of dirty jade. He might even have described her as beautiful if it weren't for the malice and hatred that radiated from her. Suddenly, the woman began to smile, and her mouth was split from ear to ear in such a malevolent grin Simon's heart was seized with dread.

Simon stared, transfixed by the woman's snow-white, pupilless eyes. Her face was filling the mirror now, absorbing Simon's vision completely. This was *not* the demon Andras. This was the witch, Aida Merryck.

Her mouth opened wider, like the gaping portal to the abyss. Her eyes became slits that pierced Simon's being and penetrated the very depths of his soul, and a guttural roar emanated from her in a long-sustained scream that no human lungs could ever endure. The roar filled Simon's being like the violent crashing of waves upon a cold and desolate shore. From her mouth began to seep an inky black liquid that flowed towards Simon like the tendrils of an octopus, enshrouding him in an icy cold veil, suffocating him. The adrenaline was overwhelming, yet he couldn't pull himself away. His eyes locked with Merryck's as she took possession of him.

Simon could feel his self being filled with a cold, black iciness. He could feel himself losing his physical body to Merryck, which was now becoming merely a vessel to this ancient evil. Then, suddenly, he felt his body stand bolt upright. Paralyzed, with no control over his limbs, Simon was now just a mere passenger in his body as it crashed violently, headfirst, into the hardwood floor, slicing a jagged gash open on his right temple. Blood gushed onto the floor as he futilely struggled to regain control of his limbs. Feeling overwhelmed and defeated, Simon powerlessly observed what was unfolding, locked away inside his mind, his body riddled by the powerful abyssal parasite.

Whilst he could not control his body, he could feel everything that was happening to it: the frantic racing of his heart, the nausea in the pit of his stomach, and the violent spasms of his limbs that he fought desperately to control to no avail.

More fear and confusion assailed Simon as his right hand involuntarily reached forward to grip the floor violently, fingernails shattering down to the fleshy nail beds as his hands clawed at the floorboards to pull his body forward. With horror, Simon observed as his body slowly clawed its way towards the open fireplace, his fractured mind unable to comprehend what was happening. The flames of the roaring fireplace writhed and flickered before him, taking on a most unusual aspect as though in slow motion. Simon can feel the dry heat getting closer, building with sickening intensity.

As Merryck's intention became clear, Simon screamed internally. His upper body rose so that his left hand clutched the searing hot metal of the brass fireplace, his hand hissing as the skin on his palm sear as he pulled his body towards the roaring flames.

There is a moment of relief when his body lurched suddenly to the left, away from the roaring fire, but this is only short-lived as Simon's hands seized the large jar of sulphuric acid from the display cabinet next to the fireplace. Fingers scrambled frantically at the lid, like the convulsions of a dying tarantula, trying to prize open the seal. Shaking arms lifted the heavy container over his head to dowse his body with the vicious liquid.

The pain immediately overwhelmed Simon as his blonde hair instantly evaporated with a disgusting hissing and sizzling sound. A sour and overpowering stench immediately filled the room around him. His eyes, nose, and mouth were instantly eaten by the searing fluid, dissolving his face to drip in viscous globs like tallow streaming down the shaft of a melting candle, destroying the physical beauty he had always possessed, robbing him of his sight and smell but leaving the ability to feel completely unaffected.

The excruciation of his liquefied eye sockets that he felt slowly seep

167

into the frontal lobe of his brain was so overwhelmingly intense that he barely felt his hands being destroyed by the acid, the ligaments constricting and fusing, forcing his fingers to curl inwards, to dissolve into misshapen stumps of melted flesh.

Simon felt vomit erupt into his throat with a painful spasm, but with his lips, tongue, and nose fused shut, there was no avenue of escape, thus forming a painful burning pressure in his throat that began to choke him. Simon's brutalized body suddenly slumped backward as the acid disfigured him beyond all recognition, sulphuric vapors coiling away from his flailing and grunting form with a sickening hissing sound as the witch Merryck released him from her cruel grasp, bored of her plaything, leaving it used, defiled, and discarded.

As his life faded, Simon felt that his very soul was being drawn out and eaten by that inky black nebulous form that now hung in the air above him. He is utterly unaware of the banging on the door or the commotion building outside his apartment or the sound of Lucy screaming his name as his life slips away, devoured by the witch to feed her dark spirit.

Outside Simon's apartment, Lucy had been unable to understand why he didn't answer or why there was an acrid-smelling smoke coming from under Simon's front door, the sour stench of burning human flesh. She had to fetch her driver from the street below to smash the door open, and when they both poured into that smoke-filled room, quickly followed by a gathering of horrified residents, the sight before her was impossible to comprehend.

The figure of a burnt man with melted stumps for hands and a head lay convulsing violently on the floor and making the most inhuman groaning noise, like a pig being slaughtered.

"Simon!" Lucy screamed, running towards the wretched remains of the man she had loved so deeply, unable to take in the full extent of the horror before her.

She fell next to Simon's body, sobbing hysterically as her driver vainly tried to pull her away. However, Lucy was rooted to the spot and wholly transfixed on Simon's lifeless and disfigured body. So much so in fact that she did not see the shadowy substance which had lingered above seep slowly back into the black shard of obsidian.

AUTHOR BIO

A passion drives William Tudor to create dark occult-themed horror stories that blend surrealism and cosmic horror elements that test the limits of the reader's comfort zone. He holds a law degree with strong first-class honors and is the primary caregiver for his autistic son, who continues to inspire and motivate him.

LOST SLEEP

BY BERNARDO VILLELA

I.

Once upon a time, there was a boy named Amets. One night when he was but five years of age, he awoke in the night and could not fall back asleep. Amets was not very compliant about sleeping, but his father was a stickler about it. On this night, however, he had made an honest effort to return to sleep.

He sat on the staircase for a while, hiding behind the enclosing wall, hoping to escape their notice. The wall hid his body, but his footie-pajamas showed when he wiggled his toes.

His father, Iñigo, spotted him.

"Amets!" he cried, then broke into a string of chastisements in Basque.

"I woke up an hour ago, and I couldn't get back to sleep. I'm sorry!"

His mother, Zuniga, chastised her husband with series of words that Amets couldn't understand.

"No, *Mira*, I'm sorry I got carried away."

"Why does sleep matter anyway? It's so stupid," Amets protested.

"Let me tell you a little story," his father said as he escorted him back upstairs.

Zuniga knew Amets would be wary about wandering back up to where sleep had eluded him, so she followed a few steps back like a silent shadow.

Iñigo assumed the responsibility of tucking him back in, as Zuniga had laid him down to sleep earlier that evening. She stood outside and eavesdropped to listen to the story her husband would spin.

Zuniga knew the love of her life had a penchant for tales that varied in tone and interpretation to the young mind. More than once, she told her husband about the kind of stories they ought to share with their impressionable son. She would not contradict his narrative midstream, not because she agreed with antiquated misogynist notions, but because discord between them would exacerbate Amets' insomnia.

Until tonight, she had never regretted letting her husband continue unabated, but allowing this particular story to continue was something she'd lament for the rest of her life. As she watched Iñigo tell Amit this story, it felt as if the world tilted sideways, and she was watching them on a movie screen that she couldn't pause.

"Amets, I think I should tell you a story about not sleeping."

"Dad, stories have to begin with, 'Once upon a time!'"

"They do when they're made-up bedtime stories."

Iñigo saw the promise Amets showed, so he had to remind himself he was only five and avoid explaining things like genre conventions. Even though, Iñigo knew his son could understand the concept if Iñigo explained it in simple words.

"Is this a story about you?"

"No, but I heard it when I was young. It's a true story that should be told more often."

172

At this moment, Zuniga's motherly intuition was alight, and she had a sinking feeling in her gut.

You're lying to our son. God help me, Iñigo, she thought.

"Amets, there are too many parents who tell their children, '*Ai Papito*, you have to sleep because I said so,' or 'you're growing and need rest.' Kids don't care about that. They don't care when they can't see how it affects them."

"What do you mean, *Papi*?"

"Well, if I don't sleep, maybe you can see these bags under my eyes grow. But for kids, that doesn't happen very often."

Amets was still a little confused.

"And you can't see the hours of sleep you lost, but it can affect and hurt you and those around you."

"How?"

"Everybody in the world, *Mijo*, must sleep a certain amount. The world ensures the world has enough sleep available for everybody, but if you don't take all your rest, someone else gets it."

"Maybe they need it more than I do," Amets said.

Iñigo smiled at his son's wise response.

"That's true, but sometimes the world can make up for it."

"How?"

"Well, you like racing your friends to recess, right?"

Amets nodded.

"If your friend gets ahead of you, what do you do?"

"Run faster."

"Right. And if you get ahead of your friend, do you slow down?"

"No."

"Right. Sometimes the world does that with the sleep it needs to give out."

"I don't understand."

173

"Did *Mami* ever read you the story of Rip Van Winkle?"

Amets nodded.

"Well, that's not the only story of someone falling asleep for a long time. A Greek shepherd, Epimenides, fell asleep for fifty-seven years. The Seven Sleepers of Ephesus slept 200 years to avoid persecution and keep Christianity alive. Honi HaMe'agel slept seventy years. There are many other examples: Peter Klaus, The Burial Mound at Salt Knowe, Niamh, and Oisin. But what you may not realize is all these stories come from truth, *Hijo*.

"And things that don't play into stories factor in, too. For example, sleep disorders."

"What are those?"

"That's not important right now. My point is, if you don't sleep when you're supposed to, it can force another—maybe a stranger, maybe someone you love—to sleep for a long time."

Zuniga saw her son look like he was about to nod off. She decided not to say anything to her husband, and she hoped Amets would forget the awful story.

On the other hand, Iñigo was quite pleased with himself and his story. Folklore was his field of expertise and had kept him employed as an academic and professor, but he was most pleased with the speed with which he thought of his story.

As Amets drifted off to sleep, his father's story slipped into the fibers of his subconscious and stained it.

II.

What fearful symmetry, a now forty-year-old Amets thought with a shudder as he crashed into his pillow.

174

I am as old now as Dad was when he told me that story. Why? Why did I just pass it on?

It had been difficult, but Amets had not thought of that story in twenty years.

"I don't feel like sleeping! Sleeping is stupid!" his son had protested.

Caleb is five like I was.

It wasn't even Caleb's lamentation—a common refrain among children since time immemorial—that brought the story to mind.

He and his wife, Marcella, had been trying to enjoy a nightcap when their son's loud little feet thumped inelegantly down the stairs.

Amets had not even been angry that it was two hours past Caleb's bedtime. He agreed to a second shift getting Caleb to sleep, especially after Marcella's hard time getting him in the bath.

Then, when Caleb agreed to lay down, and it was story-time anew, the words just tripped Amets' tongue.

"Once upon a time, there was a boy who did not understand why he needed to sleep. The little boy convinced his mother and father that he slept every night. He always awoke refreshed in the morning, which fooled his parents. The boy's plan succeeded for a week. Then on the eighth night, he was visited by *The Nightside*."

"What's *The Nightside*?"

"Nobody knows. The boy couldn't see it because it was like a walking black hole, but that's what it called itself."

"What'd The Nightside do?"

"It took care of all things that had to do with the night."

"Isn't that the Sandman?"

"The Sandman is only concerned with dreams and sleep. The Nightside is the sandman's boss. Since this little boy had resisted the sandman's best efforts, The Nightside had to visit the boy personally."

There was a somber understanding that came over Caleb's face.

"So, The Nightside said to the boy," Amets continued. "'Child, your avoidance of sleep shall have dire consequences.'"

"How?" Caleb asked, anxiousness creeping into his voice.

"The boy asked the same question, and The Nightside responded, 'Another will be forced to sleep, either naturally or in sickness, to bring the night back into balance.' With that, the boy laid himself down and slept at last. The boy never resisted going to bed again, though he was haunted by the constant fear his parents would one day go to sleep and never awake."

Caleb showed no emotion at the story's end. But when Amets turned off the lights, Caleb didn't protest.

"Good night, son. I love you," Amets said.

Amets' heart skipped a beat until finally, his son said it back.

Amets laid in bed in disbelief, replaying the story over and over and trying to ferret out his son's true reaction.

It was now Amets who was unable to sleep.

There was a knock on the door. For the second time that night, Amets' heart stopped.

III.

In Amets' experience, stains of the subconscious took some time to come to light. Just the same, Amets' obsession with The Nightside took time to develop.

When his father initially had told him the story, the dreams he'd had that he could remember were those of candy. After, he had expected that his dreams would take a dark turn, but it was the opposite.

Though the words his father spoke never strayed from his mind, it was a few years before the well-crafted half-truths his father told him had formed into a personal mythology. Amets had found the word 'Nightside'

176

in an astronomy book, and his nubile young mind morphed it into an entity who held dominion over lost sleep and other nocturnal happenings.

His father had always had hourglasses around the house because he said a classical device was essential to the work of a folklorist. Amets believed that to be true but had a sense that wasn't the real reason his dad kept hourglasses. Amets sensed that his father was incapable of explaining the reason the sand-sifting timepiece mesmerized him. Whenever Amets would read a story, his father would use an hourglass as a timekeeper.

Amets became immersed in narrative stories. He'd discovered Washington Irving's story, then learned of other historical figures and read of them, committing the various narratives to memory. He would find the narratives sporadically through the years, and then he realized they all had a similar theme: "How not to end up like my father?"

This realization was insightful, but Amets struggled to understand it. He loved his father, even in his erudition. They had never had an unpleasant exchange. Despite his and his mother's hotheaded arguments, if Amets was destined to become like one of his parents, he chose his mother. He had this feeling from deep within since he was about eight years old when the sight of a homeless man moved both Amets and his mother to tears. If Iñigo felt anything, he swallowed it. Young Amets thought to himself, *I'm like mamá, and I'm glad.*

It would take years for Amets to realize how much, fairly or unfairly, he extrapolated from that one short interaction.

As a junior in high school, his parents began to make him think deeply about higher education. Though, they never pressured him. It wasn't until Amets was a father himself that he realized what tremendous restraint this must have taken his parents. After all, his father was a professor of anthropology, and his mother had a masters in romance languages. *The intelligentsia*, Zuniga would joke. It would have been natural and forgivable for Amets' parents to put the pressure on high. Still, Amets' parents instead focused on his natural abilities and left the decision of college up to him.

Unfortunately for Amets, he chose the wrong path, and he continued to for many years and many failures.

Then when he turned twenty-five, for reasons Amets could not explain, he began reading songs and sonnets by John Donne. Unexpectedly, memories of his father's tale came rushing back, refracted, and became a renewed focus in his life.

IV.

Amets was ripped out of his thoughts by a knock on his bedroom door. Logic dictated that Caleb knocked on Amets' bedroom door, but Amets' heart skipped a beat.

Opening the door and seeing the fear in his son's eyes did not put Amets' mind at ease.

"I had a bad dream."

"Come in," Amets said. He expected his wife to veto his invitation, but she didn't.

"Come in, Baby," Marcella said.

"It was a *terrible* dream," Caleb said.

"Do you remember it?" Amets asked.

Caleb looked to his mother as if seeking permission to speak.

"It can help to talk about it," she said, granting permission.

He inhaled, swallowing his nervousness.

"I saw sand-glasses. The sand-glass clocks floated over me."

"What's a sand-glass clock, Sweetie?" Marcella asked.

"Like Daddy has."

"Hourglasses," Amets said.

"Then there was something flying thing above the hourglasses, but I couldn't see its face," Caleb said. "Then I saw the man that dresses in all-black, the one you see at Halloween that cuts people down like corn."

"The Grim Reaper?" Marcella asked. "What does he do?"

"He's Death, in the cowl," Amets said, pantomiming a cowl.

"Yeah, and the Sandman was there."

Amets knew the Sandman in Caleb's mind was a cuter version, more akin to Wee Willie Winkie than Hoffmann's version. So at least there was a dichotomy in the dream, but Caleb was still clearly terrified.

"Was the flying one moving too fast for you to see its face, or was it too dark?" Amets asked.

"Too dark," Caleb said. "It was The Nightside, I think."

In that instant, Amets prayed silently.

One way Amets was like his parents, until recently, was his secular agnostic, almost atheist, existence. Amets' parents had left Francoist Spain in part due to the Church.

Amets liked to believe that he was similar to his parents in his strict adherence to determinism. He fought against both nature and nurture to carve his path. However, in both personal and professional regards, he found he bred unhappiness by rebelling against what could bring him joy and success.

His coming to religion was a fortunate occurrence.

Amets passed a woman drawing on a sketchpad in an art gallery one day. She was parked in front of a medieval Madonna and Child, which she was drawing. He struck up a whispered conversation with her about the statue, and she showed him her sketches. Later, over coffee, she mentioned she had ideas for children's books, but she could never find the right words to go with her illustrations.

Amets and the woman decided to collaborate on a book of hers that had previously been rejected. They were successful, and their revised version sold. They became a team, then a couple, then husband and wife, and finally, parents. God had brought them together, and Amets became a believer.

"What's The Nightside?" Marcella asked Amets pointedly.

"Caleb, why don't you lay down while I speak with your mother in the hall?" Amets said.

Caleb did as his father said. The fury in Marcella's eyes intensified.

V.

Stepping into the hallway with Marcella, Amets realized he had no idea if such a scene ever transpired between his mother and father. As a teenager, he learned to recognize his mother's version of *the look*, which said, "I won't embarrass you in front of your son, but if you think we won't be talking about this later, you're crazy." 'But at the tender age of five, Amets hadn't figured out *the look* yet, and he thought maybe his mother had just been aghast.

They must've talked about it afterward, right?

But Amets now undoubtedly saw *the look* on Marcella's face, and he knew they needed a moment alone.

"What was that about?" Marcella asked.

Sighing, Amets shared with Marcella the history of the story, adding embroidery about how much the story had frightened him.

"So why did you tell him? Why am I just hearing about this?"

"It came out. I couldn't stop myself."

"Why were you keeping this from me?"

"Even with all the time it had previously consumed me—I hadn't thought much about it since meeting you."

180

"And then just out of your mouth—"

Neither Amets nor Marcella herself knew how she was going to end that sentence, and neither ever found out.

"Mom! Dad!" Caleb shrieked. His voice sounded high-pitched and more terrified than ever before.

Throwing the door open, Amets and Marcella suddenly stopped confounded. They stared at their bed where the comforter and bedsheets were lazily floated downward through the air. As the bedding floated down, a spot of absolute blackness appeared underneath the bedding. Without warning, the bedding was vacuumed in the black hole. It was the Nightside.

VI.

"What do you mean, the *Nightside*?" Marcella asked frantically from the passenger seat. They called, no one answered, so they drove.

"It's what I call them and that place. It's all I know for sure. My dad knows more."

Marcella still couldn't believe she'd agreed to drive to her in-laws rather than calling the police or even walking around outside yelling Caleb's name.

Of course, then she remembered the sight of the covers disappearing, presumably with her son. How could that be explained to the police? It couldn't. They would never believe it, and likely she and Amets would get arrested. If Caleb ever showed up, this incident could cost them custody. No matter how well-off they were, a certain sense of impending doom festered in the heart of immigrants, especially as it related to their children.

Just because Marcella thought these things didn't stop her from crying or screaming Caleb's name as they passed darkened urban playgrounds, nor did it stop her from committing other illogical acts. She loved Amets for not chiding her.

As Amets was about to bang on the door of his parents' apartment, nerves seized Marcella again.

"What if they're asleep?" she asked, as if in an emergency it mattered.

Amets banged on the door.

Iñigo, now an octogenarian, answered the door.

"What's wrong, Son?" Iñigo asked, and Amets told his father. The expected shock and panic was followed by, "*Llama la policía!*"

"Dad, I can't. He vanished right before our eyes!"

"How could that be?"

"It's my fault. It probably happened because I told Caleb about the Nightside."

"*¿Que?*" Iñigo asked.

"Didn't I tell you—" Zuniga began to lecture Iñigo.

"Zuniga, I never said anything like this! I never named them! I never thought he'd remember. So your son disappears, and you come to lay a guilt trip on me?"

"No, Dad, we came because we need more information."

"What do you mean?"

"I still remember the story you told me when I was five. That led to the story I told Caleb."

"You're the storyteller, not me. I always knew that," Iñigo said.

"Yeah, but there must be other things you know that can help! We could never have anticipated this."

"*Hijo*, if the story is true and these things that keep sleep and wakefulness in balance are actually real, then rules and science will be of no help to you. I have never done well with physics, but even if Einstein had all the answers, it wouldn't help you. These things have Caleb...."

"Where did you first find the story?"

182

"It was thirty years—"

"Forty years ago, and if I can remember, so can you."

"I've always been good at connecting themes in folklore. At that moment that you couldn't sleep, it just came to me. Do you remember how you named the things?" Iñigo asked.

"Yes. I envisioned the dark side of a planet, a dark half that would counterbalance the light half. The evil side of sleep."

"I keep thinking about the story of the Seven Sleepers, Son. They slept, and maybe they slipped into another timeline—"

"Are you saying you think Caleb has slipped into another timeline?" Marcella asked.

"Dad, I thought you said physics wasn't your thing?"

"It's just a guess. It's also possible these things, whatever they are, don't appreciate being vilified."

"Then why take Caleb? Why not *me*?"

"To punish you."

"But I wouldn't have known—"

"No, but think about it. All I said was they created balance, but you made them into terrors."

Amets' swallowed hard. He knew his father was right.

Together, they returned home, hoping this was just a nightmare and their son had miraculously reemerged. Amets was worried about his wife's reaction. She'd been reticent and red-faced.

Will this be the end of us? he wondered.

"We're almost there," he said as if she didn't know the way to their building.

"Why are we blindly believing your father?" she suddenly blurted. "He's blaming five-year-old you. And you're just taking it. Do *you* blame Caleb?"

Without responding, Amets hung a left and pulled onto their block. He hadn't expected her to go after his father.

"Why is Caleb gone? Your father told you a story he claimed was real, but it didn't involve people vanishing, just sleeping."

"He has a point, though. I was the one who named the entities, and I gave them their intent."

"You dressed up a story your father told you."

Amets parked the car.

"He lied to you," she concluded.

"But the story is real. Perhaps, Dad just doesn't know all the facts."

"You didn't create these things that kidnapped Caleb."

He opened the door.

"Amets!" she shouted. "Do we even have a plan?"

"No. I just know we can't keep leaning on stories."

"Jesus, Amets! We must do something!" Marcella said in frustration after the couple searched the apartment and still couldn't find Caleb. Marcella wasn't surprised, just worried and frustrated.

"We're going to do something," Amets said as he pulled a bottle of brandy from the fridge.

"How is *that* supposed to help?" Marcella demanded.

He plucked two snifters from the cabinet and headed toward their bedroom. Jaw dropped, Marcella followed him. He set the glasses and bottle down on a bedside table, then went into the bathroom and returned with a pill bottle.

"That's a suicide mission," she said, recognizing her sleeping pills. Amets stared at her in silent determination. She nodded, took the bottle from his hand, and portioned them each a pill.

"This works fast enough without the booze, she said."

"I love you," he said.

Together, they swallowed the pills.

184

Amets waded through the aether. Caleb was nowhere to be found, but he allowed himself a sigh of relief at the sight of Marcella. She was sleeping.

Are we in separate dreams? he wondered.

Without warning, purple, blue, silver, and gray pulses of color pierced the darkness. Amets searched for the source of the flashes, but he deciphered none.

Turning around, Amets jumped at the sudden appearance of a cadaverine figure wrapped in chains. It was an androgynous vision of evil, an antithesis of Jacob Marley. Unsure where the knowledge was born, Amets knew this must be the sandman. There was a dull clicking as the sandman tapped his long, uncut nails together.

From the spot she'd been laying, Marcella looked up just in time to see the sandman raise his hand and a group of hourglasses appearing in the blackness that surrounded them. Amets focused on the hourglasses. There were hundreds, perhaps thousands, of them.

They go clockwise, Amets remembered Caleb whispering to him.

As foreseen, the hourglasses began to spiral and move, creating a funnel of time.

Probably twenty-four tiers, Amets thought.

The hourglasses ominously spun in place, then dove, and one by one crashed into a sleeper on the ground. They broke open, burying the child in sand.

"Caleb!" Marcella called out. Suddenly, Amets recognized the sleeper.

"Caleb!" Amets called, adding his voice to Marcella's shouts.

Amets and Marcella ran through the inky nothingness, vertigo threatening to overturn them. It felt like they'd never get there.

185

"You!" a booming voice shouted. Amets turned, expecting the sandman, but this was a horror much greater. Behind him, was the embodiment of darkness and oblivion. It was the Nightside.

"You have stolen from me!" the creature yelled.

Amets saw how close he and Marcella were to Caleb. He turned to Marcella.

"Take him and go!" he shouted.

"But—"

"I'll manage," he interrupted her. "It's me it wants."

Tears in her eyes, she turned and ran the rest of her way to Caleb, unable to fight her maternal instinct. Amets watched as she dug her hands into the sand and pulled Caleb out. He saw Marcella wrap herself around Caleb's body, then check for signs of life. Seemingly satisfied, Marcella got up with Caleb in her arms and ran into the darkness.

Amets knew she would not look back. It was an unspoken agreement between them. *Save Caleb.*

Marcella woke up in bed, eye to eye with Caleb, who was rubbing the sleep from his eyes. She clutched her son and sobbed.

Wait, Amets! she thought, pushing herself up to check on Amets.

She smiled, seeing him in the same place she'd seen him fall asleep, but the smile quickly faded. She could not wake him.

Days passed, and Marcella realized the Nightside was holding Amets. She worried he would never return to her and Caleb.

When Amets' eyes finally fluttered open, the first thing he saw was Marcella, in the perch she had created by his bedside. The first thing he noticed was her head of silver hair.

Has she been coloring her hair and not telling me? he thought, trying to blink off the dregs of sleep that pulled at him.

It was a few moments before he noticed the heart monitor and the tall, dark-haired man wearing an NYU sweatshirt.

"How long has it been?" he croaked.

Everybody stared at him, their tongues frozen by shock. Finally, a nurse whose name tag read, "Donna," broke the silence.

"Oh my God, Mr. Jimenez! I'm paging the doctor!" Donna left to do her task, her steps urgently clicking on the linoleum.

Tears brimmed in Amets' eyes as he began to realize the lost time, and everything contained within it. A man stood at the end of the bed, gripping Marcella's hand tightly.

"Amets, this is your son," Marcella said, nudging the man forward. "It's been twenty years. We're both so happy you're finally home." Her voice broke, and she joined Caleb in embracing Amets.

The nightmare was finally over.

AUTHOR BIO

Bernardo Villela has published a novella, *The Isle of Helyr,* and three short story collections: *The Bloodmaster Trilogy, Teenage Death Songs Vol. 1, and Teenage Death Songs Vol. 2.* Further, he has short fiction featured in periodicals such as *Coffin Bell Journal, The Dark Corner Zine, Constraint 280,* and forthcoming in *Rive.* He's also had stories published in anthologies such as *101 Proof Horror, A Monster Told Me Bedtime Stories, From the Yonder II,* and forthcoming in *Disturbed* and *42 Stories,* among others. He has had poetry published by *Entropy, Zoetic Press,* and *Bluepepper,* and others. You can read more about these works and various other pursuits at miller-villela.com.

THE UNTAMED

BY TOSHIYA KAMEI

Satsuki's horse stumbled and fell, hurling her out of the saddle. As she landed and skidded across the sand, the beast fell on top of her, its leaden weight pinning her down. She grimaced as a sharp pain shot through her. Despite being dead for a few weeks, she wasn't immune to physical suffering.

Her plain peach kimono with her family crest on it, her satin obi tied around her waist, and her worn-out zori were full of dust. But that was the least of her worries.

"Ow," Satsuki groaned, gritting her teeth. She tasted dusty grit in her mouth. When she tried to spit the grains out, no saliva was left in her mouth. After much struggle, she freed herself from underneath her horse. She staggered to her feet and dusted off her kimono. Contrary to the popular belief back home in footless ghosts, most ghosts walked on their feet.

A solemn silence hovered over the desolate landscape, broken only by her irregular breathing. When she was alive, only a fortnight ago, she hadn't expected ghosts to breathe like humans. Still, with the desolate

189

landscape as her witness, she swore vengeance against Colonel Pinkerton for the umpteenth time.

An almost intact skeleton clad in a tattered Confederate uniform lay half buried in the sand. Satsuki kicked off her zori and put on the soldier's leather boots. She fumbled around inside the dead soldier's coat and found a rusty canteen and a Colt 36. She slipped them into her satchel.

A few years earlier, the Civil War had ended in an awkward truce. The state of Calisona never entered the Union and largely managed to maintain the appearance of neutrality. Still, its otherwise morally upright statesmen turned a blind eye to the illegal slave trade whenever mysterious sources replenished their bank accounts.

Dust. So much dust. Her lungs were full of dust. Occasional gusts raised dust across the sun-kissed desert. The sand shifted beneath her feet, erasing her footprints. Her breathing became increasingly difficult. Fatigue blurred her eyesight. She cursed her fate. Besides her remarkable endurance of hunger and fatigue, being dead wasn't that great. The one perk she valued most, however, was the chameleon-like ability to fade into the background.

No one was in sight. Satsuki sighed. Stony mountains loomed beyond the desert carpeted with flowering cacti.

"Get up, horsey." But the animal failed to obey her commands. She grabbed its neck and tried to raise it in vain. The horse neighed weakly and stopped moving. Above her head, a flock of vultures circled, uttering blood-curdling croaks. Yellow, her canine companion, looked up and growled. Satsuki clicked her tongue. Her mouth felt dry again. She took out the canteen, twisted the cap, and took a sip. The metallic drink burned her mouth. She grimaced, spat the water out, and coughed, watching as the scorched sand absorbed the liquid.

"Go easy," Yellow said. After her death, Satsuki gained the ability to talk to certain animals. Having mastered dog language, she'd been working on the horse vernacular.

Satsuki remained silent.

"What did I tell you? You should've gotten yourself a steam horse."

"Hey, your hide is useless." Satsuki teased Yellow. "You wouldn't have even gotten me a steam pony."

"Don't be mean." Yellow feigned horror. "You wouldn't sell me, would you?"

"Don't push your luck."

Satsuki walked on, with Yellow following close behind her. She almost tripped in the oversized boots, but she had no other choice but to go on.

A few days later, they reached a railroad track.

"Let's follow this," Satsuki said. "It must lead somewhere. Hopefully, some town close to Coppertown." Rippling water mirages shimmered and faded as they trod along the tracks snaking across the barren land.

Night fell, and the stars fluttered in the sky. The temperature dropped like lead in water. Who knew ghosts felt cold? Satsuki had no idea. Silence intensified until Satsuki gathered dry weeds and started a fire. Under the flames, the weeds made popping sounds. The colonel's shining barrel flooded back to her mind. The shock of getting shot still lingered inside her.

"Satsuki, wake up." Something hot and wet slithered across Satsuki's cheek. She stirred and got up. "Do you hear that?" Yellow asked. In the distance, steam hissed. The rails shook under her feet. The whirring noises grew louder.

A black dot appeared and grew into a steam locomotive, belching clouds of black smoke and white steam. Before the train reached a curve, it slowed down. Satsuki ran along, held Yellow under her arm, and climbed up the side of a carriage onto the roof.

"We'll stay up here." Satsuki tossed a few treats toward Yellow.

"Don't fall off." Images of her death flashed before her eyes. Dying twice meant a ticket straight to Purgatory. With her untied obi, she tied herself onto the roof. The arid landscape sped past them.

After a couple of days, the locomotive screeched to a standstill. A rusty metal sign said, "Coppertown, Pop. 543."

This is it—lucky us.

Satsuki crept off the roof. Yellow followed her. It was a makeshift train depot.

"Hey, stranger," a young Confederate soldier said, chewing tobacco. "What brings you here?" His dark beard barely disguised his youthful face. "As you can see, there's not much to see. We used to mine copper here. Until the colonel found something else to mine."

"I'm looking for my brother." Satsuki's voice revealed her frustration. She pulled out a flier printed with Hiroshi's likeness. On her trek across the desert, she had folded and unfolded the paper so many times her brother's face was a blur. In the dusty dark, with his image close to her face, her tears had smeared the ink.

"Sorry." He frowned. "If he's one of the folks Colonel Pinkerton brought here several days ago, it may be too late. There's nothing you can do about it."

"What do you mean?" The mere mention of his name made her blood boil.

"Oh, you don't want to get mixed up with the colonel."

"Tell me. I must know." She seized the soldier's wrist, and he flinched. In her grip, his wrist was thinner than she'd imagined. As frail as her own.

Oh, I must look mad. Mad and dirty.

But she was sick of soldiers. Sick of their condescending eyes. Sick of the rotten color of their uniforms and their smug responses. She wanted answers, and she tightened her grip on his wrist. Answers. She'd squeeze them out of him if she had to.

192

"He's my brother," she said.

"He's digging uranium." The soldier swallowed and stepped back when Satsuki finally let go of him.

"Uranium?" She frowned. The word meant nothing to her, but a feeling of nameless dread shot through her.

"Don't ask me what it is. Chemistry is not my strong suit. The colonel says it's a new source of energy. He's got some evil scheme or such. Stick around, and you'll find out soon enough." The soldier paused to spit his tobacco and missed the spittoon. "'Scuse me. By the way, my name's Pepe. What's yours?" He wiped his hand on his pant leg then extended it to shake hers.

"I'm Satsuki." She bowed instead of shaking his hand. "Pleased to meet you."

"Where are you staying? Don't tell me you plan to camp out. My conscience prevents me from sending you to a vermin-infested inn." Pepe smiled. "Come to my place. You could use some freshening up."

"Why are you helping me?" Satsuki tilted her head.

"Can you keep a secret?" Pepe looked her in the eye, and she nodded. "The governor sent me here to keep an eye on the colonel. I joined his regimen to get close to him. When I swore my allegiance to him, I used my copy of *Don Quixote* instead of Pinkerton's Bible." He flashed a mischievous smile, and looked heavenward, and crossed himself.

"What are you talking about?"

"His cursed Bible. It binds people."

Satsuki remained silent, puzzled.

"But I'm not authorized to do anything else." Pepe blew out a breath to punctuate his words. "My boss finds the colonel useful. But politics is beyond me. It bores me."

"Can you help me find my brother?"

"You can't go peek in every mine in town. Give me some time to

193

gather information. Once I discover the mine your brother works, I'll take you to him."

Pepe carried her bag through an unpaved, dirt street as Yellow curled up in her arms. As they walked past faded-looking buildings, she saw sooty, half-naked children making a ruckus. Left to their own devices, the children fought for candy. Their laughter sounded like donkeys braying.

"Here we are! Home, sweet home." Pepe sing-songed and pointed to a two-story brick house with a small porch at the front. Creeper vines crawled over its walls. The porch floor creaked as they walked inside.

Satsuki followed him upstairs. "Look, this is your room." Pepe ushered her in. "Check my sister's wardrobe. Her clothing may not be your style, but please help yourself to anything you fancy." Pepe smiled. "I thought you might want to freshen up a bit."

"Oh, thank you. She wouldn't mind?"

"She wouldn't mind." He looked down. "She's dead now."

"I'm sorry."

The following morning, Satsuki found herself alone in the house. Pepe had left to gather more information about Hiroshi while she was asleep. After a light breakfast, a feverish restlessness seized her. Like a fenced-in horse, she paced from one side of the room to the other. Staying put wasn't an option, so she marched outside with a spring in her step. The porch floor neighed ominously under her feet. There, with his eyes closed, Yellow lay still, pooped in the blazing hot sun. He swatted occasional flies with lazy flicks of his tail.

"I'll see you in a bit." With no destination in mind, Satsuki hurried toward town. When she passed by a small farmhouse, she noticed the woman following her. Slim as a toothpick, she wore a shiny blue rebozo draped over her thin shoulders. The weight of her gaze drew Satsuki in. The woman beckoned and invited Satsuki inside her house.

"My husband hasn't come home for weeks." María poured Satsuki

194

a cup of tea. "We have a baby on the way. At first, I thought he just picked up a few extra hours at the mine." María touched her stomach and rubbed its bulge. "If it's a boy, we'll name him Jorge, after his papá." María turned to a framed photograph of her husband on the windowsill, grabbed it, and held it against her chest. The kitchen was sweltering, but Satsuki let the sweat gather on her brow.

Another family was torn apart by the cruelty of men. Satsuki fought to control her rage. The encounter with María only hardened her resolve. More than ever, she was determined to take vengeance. She said goodbye and headed back to Pepe's house.

Satsuki sat on a sun-faded wicker chair that squeaked as she shifted her weight. While she rocked back and forth, mulling over what María said, a cloud of dust bloomed in the distance, the sound of drumming hoof beats grew louder, and a white horse emerged. Its rider carried a mail pouch. The rider stopped her horse and tipped her hat. Back home, she had never seen a woman delivering letters.

"You've got mail, Ma'am." She handed Satsuki an inoffensive-looking envelope.

"Oh, very kind of you." By reflex, Satsuki bowed and reached for the letter. As soon as she received it, the rider tipped her hat again, kicked her horse's sides with her heels, and trotted away across the prairie. With a "Pony Express" stamp affixed, the letter was from Texas and addressed to "Miss Josefina Perez."

"Who is Josefina? I thought his sister was dead." Satsuki held the letter against the blistering afternoon light.

"Beats me." Yellow half opened his eyes, flapping his ears to dislodge the flies. "Why don't you ask him?"

"I hate prying. I don't want him to think I'm a busybody."

"If you say so." Yellow closed his eyes again.

"How do I look, Pepe?" Satsuki twirled, and her hand-me-down dress swung. Her steps were as light as the cheerful tune she hummed. Her head was erect as she set the table. The smell of fresh-baked bread and chicken soup filled the kitchen-cum-dining room.

"You look mighty fine if you will allow me to say so. That dress was my sister's favorite."

"But it's rather constraining." Her corset creaked as she breathed. "How can I breathe in this thing? Why can't I dress like you?" She pointed to Pepe's cotton shirt and pants.

"Do as you please. It's a free country. Or so it was the last time I checked."

As Satsuki put her fork down on the table, she glanced at Pepe. He wore a serene expression as he thumbed through the newspaper. Did she want to blemish that? Still, curiosity surged within her. She cleared her throat, feeling embarrassed by her duplicity before she even spoke.

"Say, who is Josefina?"

Pepe looked taken back by the abruptness of her question, but he quickly recovered and said nothing. He gazed afar as though reminiscing about something unpleasant.

"This came in the mail today." Satsuki took the letter out of her pocket and placed it on the table in front of him. "It's your sister, correct? I thought she was dead. What's going on?"

"It's a long story. Anyway, let's eat before the food gets cold." He gestured for her to sit on the other side of the table. "Mamá thinks my sister's still here."

"You mean she doesn't know she's dead?" She absentmindedly held her spoon. She wasn't hungry.

"No." He dipped a piece of bread into his soup. "Not exactly."

"How is it possible? You're not going to tell her?"

"Well, as I said, it's complicated." Pepe wore a quaint, shy smile.

196

"When Colonel Pinkerton arrived, he enslaved everybody." On one side of a ridge, an adit stood ajar. Pepe explained that the colonel's guards played poker on their breaks. Pepe's uniform gave him easy access to anywhere in town.

"While the minors work in precarious conditions, many are injured and killed. So, he brings immigrants to replace them."

With her lantern in her hand, Satsuki followed Pepe inside. The wood-lined walls seemed to close in on Satsuki as they advanced through a horseshoe-shaped tunnel. The sounds of picks and shovels traveled. Satsuki fought the urge to cower and cling to Pepe.

The moist air in the dimly lit mine suffocated Satsuki. If she had been alone, she would have screamed in panic, but Pepe's presence helped her maintain her calm. When Satsuki waved her lantern, ghostly figures emerged out of the penumbra and hovered before her. Equipped with mining gear, the enchanted miners toiled nonstop like locomotive engines. By sheer luck, she spotted Hiroshi. Tears fell as she ran to him. But she didn't care because it was dark. This was her brother—her flesh and blood. If she could only get him out of there, he would return to his former self. She was sure of it. Still, there was something amiss with him. As she skidded to a halt, the smile fading from her lips, she sensed something was terribly wrong. His eyes were devoid of light. He didn't see her.

"Hey, Hiroshi. What are you doing?" She grabbed his shoulders and shook them. "I've been looking all over the place for you."

Hiroshi didn't respond. Instead, he pushed her away and went back to wielding his pick against the rock wall before him.

Satsuki turned to Pepe. "What's wrong with him? He seems to be under a spell."

"It's no use." Pepe shook his head. "You see how he is. He's enchanted." He grimaced. "Sorry, Satsuki. He's a goner. Pinkerton put a spell on the miners. Doctor Chu says there's no cure. They can't be freed.

Unless you—"

"There's a saying, 'To kill a snake, cut off its head.'"

"It's too dangerous. Well, some say the colonel is the devil himself."

"I don't care." Satsuki swallowed back the words she wanted to yell out: *I'm already dead anyway.*

Satsuki proposed a duel with the colonel, though she shivered at the thought. She didn't want to die twice. No thanks. Purgatory was the last place she wanted to be. Eternal suffering. The mere thought gave her chills. But she had to save her brother.

To Satsuki's surprise, the colonel agreed. Captain Smith said the colonel needed some diversion from the day-to-day operation of the mines. Pepe warned her that the colonel would lay a trap for her, that he was up to no good, but she wouldn't take no for an answer. As far as she was concerned, killing him was the only way to break the colonel's spell and save her brother. She slipped out of Josefina's dress, wiggled into Pepe's pants, and set out alone.

Their duel was to take place at noon. The weapon would be the sword. Out of habit, Satsuki showed up early and hid. There was no sign of the colonel. When the sun reached the zenith, the only saloon in town was already open, beckoning thirsty drunkards. The joint belonged to the colonel's brother-in-law. From time to time, Satsuki gazed at the clock in front of Town Hall. Time crawled slowly, and a spider tumbled down from the eaves onto her neck. When the clock hands indicated noon, several soldiers on horses appeared like a herd of centaurs. She recognized a mustached man in his uniform leading the pack.

"How have you been, Colonel?" Satsuki stepped into the sun.

"So nice of you to ask." The colonel smiled and touched his mustache. "I was just doing fine. Until some mare showed up in town uninvited. I suppose some of them have to be tamed more than once." The colonel tipped his hat.

"Some mares may be too much for you, Colonel."

"You haven't learned your lesson, have you?" The colonel shook his head with mock dismay. "That's too bad. You should've stayed dead. You'll regret this. I promise you." He made fists with the gloves on his hands.

"This time, it'll be different." She paused a moment to gather her wits and hide her fear. "You'll see."

"What makes you say that? You're a fool!" He bellowed. "We haven't got all day. Let's get on with it." The colonel turned to his right-hand man.

"Captain Smith." The captain brought forward two identical swords. The colonel spat and beat his gloved hands together. He glared at Satsuki, seized one, and drew it. Satsuki followed suit.

The swords hissed through the air and flickered like snake tongues. Orange sparks flew out where the blades met. Gritting her teeth, Satsuki wielded her sword at the colonel's chest, only to have him step aside. They closed in on each other, swords crossed, and beads of sweat gathered on their brows. When she faced Colonel Pinkerton up close, close enough that she could feel his tobacco-stained breath on her cheek, she didn't see passion or heat in his green, lizard gaze. Instead, what she saw was reptilian calculation. The dull sound of their boots on the dry dirt contrasted with the zing of steel against steel.

A bullet hissed through the air. Satsuki felt pain in her hand and dropped her sword to the ground. She looked up and saw the captain holding his gun. He leered at her. A wisp of blue smoke rose from the end of the barrel.

"Satsuki!" She heard Pepe's voice. He tossed her revolver to her, and she caught it with one hand. She cocked her gun and aimed at the colonel. The bullet entered right between his eyes and passed out the back of his head. The colonel fell with a loud thud.

Several shots rang out. Satsuki ducked out of instinct. Weapons in their hands, a crowd burst out of the general store. María led the group, pointing her shotgun at the soldiers. The townspeople chanted, "We're free!"

When Satsuki caught her gaze, María signaled her to step aside. Dust flew up in clouds, and neighs and screams filled the air. The soldiers got on their horses and fled in a hurry. The fighting was over. Satsuki turned to seek Pepe out with a smile on her face and saw him buckle like a ragdoll, his face twisted into a grimace.

"Pepe!" Satsuki ran and embraced him. "I told you to stay out of this. It was between him and me." Satsuki felt her white blouse becoming soaked with blood. Pepe's blood.

"But I couldn't just let you go alone." He visibly fought to form words through quivering lips. A gob of blood welled up in the corner of his mouth and oozed down one side of his chin. "You needed me." His faint smile died away, and the light faded out of his eyes.

"I could've handled him by myself." She clicked her tongue. "Are you alright?" When she glanced toward the celebrating crowd, she saw María embracing Jorge. They kissed.

"No, I'm afraid not. They got me." Pepe bitterly smiled. His eyes narrowed. He threw up more blood. "Now your brother has been freed from the colonel's curse. Send him my regards, won't you?"

"Oh, Pepe." She felt the blood drain out of her body. "I'm sorry."

"Don't be. It's not your fault." He trembled, his lips turning blue. "I'm getting cold. I can't move my hands. Please, hold me."

Satsuki cradled Pepe's head in her arms.

"You know there's something I didn't tell you. I haven't got a sister."

"No, don't talk. Don't." Satsuki shushed. "Save your strength. Use it to wish yourself back. Like I did."

"No. There's something I've gotta tell you."

Satsuki squeezed Pepe's hand and felt his life slipping away. His blood soaked her dress. His eyes turned glassy.

"I like you. I do. I used to be like you. *A lot* like you."

"I don't care." Satsuki tenderly kissed Pepe.

"You can have all my dresses now." He smiled weakly. "I don't need them anymore."

"Thank you."

"I couldn't throw them away 'cause Mama made them for me. Promise me one thing. Get me out of this uniform before I'm buried. I don't want to be buried in this. You know I'm not like them."

"Shush. Don't worry. I know." Satsuki hummed a melancholy lullaby while caressing his hair. Tears rolled down her cheeks, reached her chin, and gleamed like shooting stars.

"He was brave," Satsuki mumbled as Hiroshi threw another shovelful of dirt over the shallow pit. "I miss him. I couldn't have saved you without his help." She looked at Hiroshi. "You'd have liked him."

"He may come back like you," Hiroshi said.

"I hope so. He'd better. I'll pester him until he does." Satsuki chuckled and laid orange blossoms in his grave. "I know he can hear us." Even ghosts hoped. And desired. As far as Satsuki could tell, they hardly differed from humans in that regard.

She squinted against the blinding sun and wiped her forehead with the back of her hand, leaving smears of dirt and sweat behind.

Author Bio

Toshiya Kamei is a fiction writer who writes in both English and Spanish. His short fiction has been published with *New World Writing*, *Revista Korad*, and *SmokeLong en Español*. His short story, "No Kisses Goodnight," was reprinted in the anthology *Insignia 2021: Best Asian Fiction*.

For more information, please visit ToshiyaKameiWrites.Wordpress.*com*

STONE AND WOOD

BY SERGIO PALUMBO

"He is gone on the mountain,
He is lost to the forest,
like a summer-dried fountain,
when our need was the sorest...." – Sir Walter Scott

The verses of Sir Walter Scott flowed in the young woman's mind as she walked along the path. That author was one of her favorite classical poets and novelists, and her love of his poetry contributed heavily to her love of Scotland, the country Scott had been born. Neala frequently vacationed there, in Scotland, traveling north to south, exploring all the countryside. She had seen nearly the whole country, and so she was excited to be visiting a forest she hadn't yet seen.

With its ancient pines and spectacular mountain scenery, the Caledonian Forest was one of Scotland's most famous landscapes, not much different from the Highlands or the stunning northern and eastern islands. The forest is said to have once covered a large part of Scottish country, and it took its name from ancient Romans who called Scotland, *Caledonia*, which meant 'wooded heights.'

That was the official name, but the locals called the forest, *the rustling woods*. Some believed the forests were called that because the leaves whispered and rustled in the wind, but others thought the name was rooted in ancient legend.

The forest was once a vast, ancient wilderness of Scots pines, birches, and other native plants, but now it was just a shadow of its previous glory. Regardless, you could easily spot some notable birds and other wildlife species, including feral European goats, squirrels, wild horses, and wolves. Luckily for these creatures, much of the surviving forest was either too steep or too rocky to be agriculturally valuable, and that was why it had been left alone over the centuries.

But hidden amid the forest, there was a set of gray, stone stairs. They were tucked away in the middle of a clearing, surrounded by trees. They were just lonely, strange stone stairs that seemed to lead to nowhere. The stairs were not on any map, and the authorities, if asked, would state the stories of the secret stairs were just myths. But there they were, right in front of Neala.

Staring at the staircase, Neala thought it looked like their shape had been cut to fit a house that wasn't there. Yet, it was rumored there had never been a house—just the stairs.

Occasionally, spring and summer tourists stumbled across the staircase while hiking through the woods, or in the winter, a local would re-discover them while hunting. But, unlike the tourists, the locals knew better than to climb the stairs.

Some reports indicated that approaching or climbing the stairs gave visitors confusion or vertigo. Some people had reported suddenly losing direction. Doctors who worked the emergency room in the local hospital had treated the wounds of many foreigners who had reported climbing the staircase, and they claimed there was an increase in cases every year.

It was also said that time didn't affect the stairs, or possibly, somebody secretly maintained them. Weeds and nearby vegetation often appeared to be trimmed back, and the steps were always free of leaves and debris. But nobody had ever spotted a caretaker.

Over time, the stairs became one of the many legends and fabled places of Scotland. Some didn't believe the stories, while others didn't dare to question their existence.

It was late morning, while on her way from Strathspey when the 28-year-old Irish tourist, Neala Ó Tadhgàin, had decided to explore the woods and by chance, found herself at the bottom of the stairs looking up. Her hand pushed her medium-length blonde curls from her eyes to have a better look. The shock she felt was slowly replaced with curiosity as she remembered tales she had heard in the village and a small, side paragraph in her travel book. She almost hadn't seen the paragraph, with its small print, buried under a section on local lores and legends.

She pieced together what she had learned about the forest. She knew it was reputed to have been the site of one of King Arthur's battles, and it had been reported that a legendary figure succumbed to madness and retreated to these woods after the Battle of Arfderydd in the year 573. According to her travel book, that tidbit had been discovered written in Middle Welsh in two Merlinic poems. Other figures in history from varied tales hinted about a close association between the forest and people who had retreated into it due to a strange madness.

But those were all just stories, Neala thought.

The morning hadn't been different than any other morning, except for her discovery of the paragraph and her decision to explore the forest. She had dressed appropriately a waterproof jacket, performance leggings, and comfortable sneakers designed for trips off the beaten path. She carried a small knapsack with a few essential items for her short hike. Neala was an accomplished hiker, reflected in her slender, muscular figure. She was well-prepared for a day of exploring the woods.

Pulled by curiosity and impulsiveness, she approached and

ascended the steps. Apprehension crept through her mind and wrapped her body in an icy grip. Then, as suddenly as it had begun, the fear evaporated.

I've already gone this far, she thought, continuing to climb even as her legs began to ache. Finally, she reached the top and gasped.

The forest had disappeared, replaced by stone arches and walls that surrounded her. Even though the stonework seemed solid, there was an unearthly uncertainty ebbing in the nearby atmospheric layers.

Neala stepped off the last step into a room with polished wooden flooring that ran wall to wall. Along the side, walls hung ancient wall lamps that lit up the entire room with ghastly brilliance. The far end of the room was furnished with a long bookshelf and curio cabinet, and small tables and countertops littered the room. Displayed on the tables were clusters of strange objects in various colors and shapes.

Kitchenware, maybe? Neala wondered. *What is this? A dream?*

Neala wandered into the room, her eyes traveling from object to object, until a noise startled her. She turned to see the shadow of a figure entering the room from a staircase that appeared to run up to a higher level.

As the figure descended, Neala was able to see they wore an embroidered yellow robe and a heavy leather belt. It appeared to be an older man, possibly about the age of eighty. His face was long but clearly defined, with a straight and prominent nose. He had heavy eyelids that hung like curtains over his emerald eyes. Deep wrinkles crossed his forehead, but he was watchful. He stared hard at Neala. But it wasn't the undaunting stare that sent shivers down Neala's spine; it was those long-pointed ears that unexpectedly jutted out of the long, white curls of his hair.

"Who are you?" Neala asked. "What is this place?"

"I'm Gowan, and this is my home. And who are you?"

"I'm Neala, a tourist... from Ireland. I discovered these steps...."

While speaking, Neala's hand searched her coat pocket. She pulled out her cell phone and looked at the screen. No signal.

"What is that? Another infernal, human contraption?" Gowan

206

asked.

"No, it's a phone. Haven't you seen a phone before?"

Gowan didn't reply. Instead, he gestured, and the phone appeared in his hand. He turned it over, scrutinizing it as if he'd never seen a phone before.

"Hey, that's mine! Give it back!" Neala yelled.

With a certain dejection, Gowan gave her phone back.

"You may have it. It seems harmless," he shrugged. Then, he looked at Neala with the same scrutinizing look he'd given the phone and said, "but tell me, how did you get past the stairs?"

"By climbing them, how else?" Neala responded, feeling flustered.

"This is unprecedented...." Gowan said, bewilderment in his eyes. Then his features became stony, and he looked at her. "Let me take a blood sample," he demanded.

"What?"

Before Neala knew what was happening, the old man moved towards her faster than her eye could see. One moment he was across the room, then he stood inches away, gripping her arm hard as he gouged a vein and stole his sample.

"Stop! Let go of me," Neala struggled, but he had already gotten what he wanted and moved towards a desk in the back. Neala stood, frozen, and watched in horror as he poured a drop of blood-her blood-onto a test strip.

His vivid eyes grew wide. "It can't be! You're a Pelling! You're one of us," he turned to look her in the eye. "I've heard some of our kind left home to go and live in the human world. It was rumored a few of them had even married some of the humans. And now here you are, half-fairy, half-human." He smiled, heavy wrinkles pushing up the corner of his twinkling eyes.

"It must be a mistake," Neala replied.

"I never make mistakes," Gowan's smile transformed into a glare.

"But fairies aren't real," Neala said, her voice quivering.

"They most definitely are. You're staring at one right now."

"Impossible," Neala objected.

"So, nobody ever told you about us? What a shame. Well, humans have called us by many names: Sluaghs, Clutterbumphs, and Glaistigs. We're masters of secluded places, lords of the free, wild environments that once stretched to all the corners of Earth. We make our homes in the thick woods across the world. Before the arrival of humans, we ruled over everything, but those days have long gone."

"I need a drink...." Neala said, averting her eyes from him.

"What may I offer you? Water, tea, herb infusions?" he asked. "I must've forgotten my hospitality."

"Alcohol would be better..." she uttered.

"I'm afraid you'll find none of that here," Gowan said. "We don't partake in that human habit."

"Maybe I just need to sit down...." Gowan nodded and motioned towards a nearby chair. Gratefully, Neala sat.

Gowan approached her with silent footsteps, and as he neared, he began speaking again.

"I imagine the world is much different than I remember. It's been such a long time since the war that separated us. Undoubtedly, human technologies and civilizations have made large strides, as usual."

"What are you talking about?" Neala asked.

"The Long Bloody War, of course."

"A war?" Neala raised her eyebrows.

"You've never heard of the war? It seems as if history has been erased." Gowan shook his head somberly.

"I've never heard of any war with fairies. Faeries are just a myth."

"I'm sad about this," Gowan turned away.

"How did it begin?" the young woman asked, sitting up like an eager student.

"It happened centuries ago. Many of the humans had begun chopping down the trees in the forest. The human population was growing too quickly, and humans took larger portions of the countryside for themselves. Prior generations of human residents lived *with* the forest, only taking what they needed. This area had been lush, wild, and free.

"But a new generation of humans took over, and the Age of Steam began. More and more men came, and more and more land they stole. They were destroying the forests. We had to stop them. So, we made a plan."

Neala leaned forward, her full attention now on Gowan. "What did you do?" She asked.

"There was a witch who lived in a secluded section of the forest. She'd been forced to leave her native village after accusations of dark sorcery, and so, she avoided other humans and wasn't interested in meddling with human affairs. But on occasion, a desperate person would seek her out for magical assistance, and she would relent. We fairies never had any issues with her, as she was quiet and kept to herself. She became just another peaceful resident of the forest.

"Then one day, the witch came to us and asked to stand before our elder. She proposed to join forces, experience, and power to resolve the problem of the other humans invading and stealing our lands. And we agreed.

"The proposal was to attack woodcutters. We would hide their tools, damage their carts, and cause illness until they left." Gowan looked down, shamefully.

"That's terrible," Neala said. "But I understand why you did it."

"Yes, but there were consequences," Gowan replied without looking up. "You see, the witch wasn't content with just driving the humans away. We didn't realize it yet, but her true plan was to rid the world of humans, forever."

"I don't understand. Did you begin killing the humans?" Neala asked.

"I, myself, did not. But the witch did, and many others of my kind followed her lead. Our forest home became stained with blood."

Neala sat in silence, trying to absorb the new information she'd learned.

"But we aren't gone. Humans still live, so you must've done something to stop it," She said.

"Eventually, the faeries recognized the evil contagion the witch had spread, and we began fighting back hatred fueled by the witch. Her magic grew stronger. She became as adept as we were at controlling the elements.

"You fought against her?"

"I did, along with other fairies...." Gowan nodded. "But there were only a few of us left. Many of our kind had already left, driven away by the war. So, when the witch attacked us, we weren't prepared. We fought bravely, but many died, including my son, Sclymgeour.

"That's not all. The witch also cursed our property. Because we had decided to betray her, refusing to fight the humans, she cast a malicious curse, sending her evil energies into our walls, and removing our protections. Our home became visible to everybody, even the humans.

"Was it the witch that killed your son?" an uncertain Neala asked him.

"Yes," Gowan sadly nodded. "I had been busy trying to re-cast another protection incantation for the house, but I was interrupted by his screams. When I turned, I saw his body on the ground, lifeless. I ran to him, overcome by grief. In my grief, I didn't return in time to complete the enchantment, and the stairs to our home remained visible. I've tried many times since, but none of the ancient arts have been effective.

"Driven by grief, regret, and rage, I sought the witch and forced her into a magical duel. I fought with all my strength, but I only managed to injure her. Soon after, she left the forest, and none of us ever saw her again."

Gowan raised his eyes and made eye contact with Neala. "But now, you're here," he said.

Neala cringed with fear. Gowan had a strange look in his eyes that sent shivers up her spine.

"You should've never entered this building, my home," Gowan said.

A strange sensation began to rise within Neala. Something wasn't right. She couldn't move her legs.

"You're going to pay for the price my people had to pay,"

Fear rose in Neala. Breathing became difficult, and her body felt weak.

"I wasn't able to remove the stair's visibility, but I was able to place a ward to prevent wandering humans from entering my home. Humans that climb the steps are cursed to experience illness, disorientation, and pain. Up until today, no human had ever made it more than halfway up the steps before they turned back. But here you are."

Neala was overcome with dizziness and nausea.

"But now it has become clear any humans of mixed descent can withstand my ward. This occurrence is frightening, indeed."

"What are you saying?" Neala's voice was weakened, and she sounded feeble. Gowan was not listening, though. He paced the room restlessly, mumbling incoherent words. Neala's words just bounced off of him and fell to the ground like bits of waste.

Gowan's bloodshot eyes were twitching with madness. Something terrible dwelled within him, and it had been awoken. There was something rotten inside him, inside his mind. After centuries of living alone, secluded in this house, fear had taken root in his soul and grown into a monster.

"I always knew somebody would eventually break the barrier, enter my home, and become a threat to me. But I expected this, so I prepared. Now, you're going to die."

211

Neala's fears became desperation, and she truly felt lost at that moment. This fairy was mad! She needed to get out of that house as soon as possible. But looking around, Neala realized the stairs that led back to the forest had disappeared

Another effect of the sorcery that was on this fairy house?

Neala sensed her strength diminishing quickly, her heart raced, and she almost lost her balance. She couldn't think clearly. She could feel the magic fogging up her mind.

She reached out to find something that she could grab for support, but she was too slow and weak. The room suddenly felt enormous and inexplicably long. The walls spread out of sight.

"Please, don't..." she begged, her voice meek.

"I had requested our four best elemental artists, renowned fairy healers, to bring my son back from death, but they wouldn't even try. They told me they *couldn't* do anything, but I knew they just refused to because of the witch.

"After his death, I sought out and killed each one of them, the way they deserved to, and then I closed myself off here, at home. Protected, safe, alone!"

His words transformed into icy gusts of wind, fueled by hatred and death. The evil whispers crept toward Neala, enveloped her with their tendrils, and began to suck the life from her body. Neala felt her true self draining from her, her pulse slowing until it came to a complete stop.

Neala's last thought was of a crazed, lonely man who had lost himself in grief. A man who had abandoned his heart to pain and fear, his spirit slowly decomposing, until all that was left was an empty shell. The thought sent a tear to Neala's eye, and the moment her heart stopped, the tear dropped.

Author Bio

Sergio Palumbo has published short stories in the *American Aphelion Webzine, WeirdYear, Quantum Muse, Antipodean SF, SQ Mag,* and 50 British Horror/Sci-Fi Anthologies, two Canadian Urban Fantasy/Horror Anthologies, and four Australian Sci-Fi Anthologies by various publishers. He is also a co-editor, together with Mrs. Michele Dutcher, of Anthologies like *Steam-powered Dream Engines, Fantastical Savannahs and Jungles, Xenobiology,* and *Bleakest Towers* published by Rogue Planet Press, an Imprint of British Horrified Press.